PENGUIN MODERN CLAS

Within the Walls

GIORGIO BASSANI was born in 1916. From 1938 onwards he became involved in various anti-Fascist activities for which he was imprisoned in 1943. His works include *The Gold-Rimmed Spectacles* and *Five Stories of Ferrara* (*Within the Walls*), which won the Strega Prize. *The Garden of the Finzi-Continis* was awarded the Viareggio Prize in 1962 and was made into a feature film.

JAMIE MCKENDRICK is an award-winning poet and translator. His translations of *The Garden of the Finzi-Continis*, *The Gold-Rimmed Spectacles* and *The Smell of Hay* are already available, and he is currently translating the rest of the Ferrara Cycle anew for Penguin Modern Classics.

GIORGIO BASSANI

Within the Walls

Translated by JAMIE MCKENDRICK

PENGUIN BOOKS

PENGUIN CLASSICS

UK | USA | Canada | Ireland | Australia
India | New Zealand | South Africa

Penguin Books is part of the Penguin Random House group of companies whose addresses can be found at global.penguinrandomhouse.com.

First published as *Cinque storie Ferraresi* 1956
Revised version first published as *Dentro le mura* 1980
First published in this translation in Penguin Classics 2016
003

Translation copyright © Jamie McKendrick, 2016

The moral rights of the author and translator have been asserted

Set in Dante MT Std 10.5/13 pt by Palimpsest Book Production Limited, Falkirk, Stirlingshire
Printed in Great Britain by Clays Ltd, St Ives plc

A CIP catalogue record for this book is available from the British Library

ISBN: 978-0-141-19216-1

www.greenpenguin.co.uk

Penguin Random House is committed to a sustainable future for our business, our readers and our planet. This book is made from Forest Stewardship Council® certified paper.

Contents

Lida Mantovani 1
The Stroll before Dinner 38
A Memorial Tablet in Via Mazzini 61
The Final Years of Clelia Trotti 92
A Night of '43 134

Lida Mantovani

1.

Turning back to the distant years of her youth, always, for as long as she lived, Lida Mantovani remembered the birth with emotion, and especially the days just before it. Whenever she thought about it, she was deeply moved.

For more than a month she had lived stretched out on a bed, at the end of a corridor, and for all that time she had done nothing but stare through the usually wide-open window opposite at the leaves of the huge, ancient magnolia which surged up right in the middle of the garden below. Then, towards the end, three or four days before her labour pains began, she had suddenly lost interest even in the magnolia's black leaves, which were shiny, as though they'd been oiled. She had even given up eating. A thing, that's what she'd shrunk into being: a kind of very swollen and numbed thing – although it was only April, it was already warm – abandoned down there, at the end of a hospital corridor.

She hardly ate anything. But Professor Bargellesi, then head of the maternity ward, would repeat that it was better that way.

He observed her from the foot of the bed.

'It's really hot,' he'd say, with those frail and reddened fingers of his smoothing his big white beard, stained with nicotine around the mouth. 'If you want to breathe as you should, it's better to keep your weight down. And anyway' – he would add, smiling – 'anyway, it seems to me you're quite fat enough already . . .'

2.

After the birth, time began to pass once more.

At first, thinking of David – irritated, unhappy, he hardly ever spoke to her, staying in bed for whole days, his face hidden under a book or else sleeping – Lida Mantovani tried to keep going on her own in the furnished room of the big apartment block in Via Mortara where she had lived with him for the last six months. But then, after a few more weeks, convinced that she'd heard the last of him, and realizing that the few hundred *lire* he'd left her were about to run out, and since, besides, her milk was beginning to run dry, she decided to return home to her mother. So in the summer of that same year, Lida reappeared in Via Salinguerra, and began once more to occupy the unattractive room, with its dusty wooden floor and its two iron beds arranged side by side, where she had spent her childhood, adolescence and the first years of her youth.

Although it had once been a carpenter's wood store, entering was by no means easy.

When you had entered the vestibule, huge and dark as a haybarn, you had to climb up by a little staircase which obliquely cut across the left-hand wall. The staircase led to a low half-door, and having passed the threshold you found your head brushing a ceiling with small beams, and were suddenly faced with a kind of well. God! How sad it all was, Lida said to herself the evening she returned home, lingering for a moment up there to look down . . . and yet, at the same time, what a sense of peace and protection . . . With the baby around her neck, she had slowly descended the steps of the inner staircase, and had made her way towards her mother, who in the meantime had lifted her eyes from her sewing, and finally leant down to give her a kiss on the cheek. And the kiss, without a single word, greeting or comment having passed between them, was returned.

Almost immediately the question of the baptism had to be confronted.

As soon as she became aware of the situation, the mother crossed herself.

'Are you mad?' she exclaimed.

While the mother spoke, anxiously declaring that there wasn't a moment to be lost, Lida felt any will to resist shrivel within her. At the maternity ward, when they had crowded around the bed to hold the baby and had excitedly asked what name she meant to give him, she suddenly thought she must do nothing *against* David, and this made her reply, No, they should hold off for a bit, she wanted to think about it for a while longer. But now, why on earth should she continue to have any scruples? What would she still be waiting for? That very evening the baby was taken to Santa Maria in Vado. It was her mother who had arranged everything, it was she who argued that he should be called Ireneo, in memory of a dead brother of whose existence Lida had never even been aware ... Mother and daughter had rushed to the church as though pursued. But, as if drained of all energy, they returned slowly along Via Borgo di Sotto, where the municipal lamplighter was doing his rounds, lighting the streetlamps one by one.

The next morning they began working together again.

Seated again as they had once been, as they had always been before, under the rectangular window which opened above them at street level, their foreheads bent over their sewing, rather than speaking of the time they had recently passed through, so bitter for both of them, they preferred, when the occasion arose, to talk of inconsequential things. They felt more closely bound together than before, much better friends. Both of them, all the same, understood that their harmony could only thus be preserved on condition that they avoided any reference to the sole topic on which their closeness depended.

Sometimes, however, unable to resist, Maria Mantovani risked a joke, a veiled allusion.

She might venture with a sigh:

'Ah, all men are the same!'

Or even:

'Men are always on the prowl – that's for sure.'

At this, having raised her head, she would stare raptly at her daughter, remembering, at the same time, the blacksmith of Massa

Fiscaglia, who, twenty years earlier, had taken her virginity and made her pregnant, remembering the rented farmhouse, hidden among the fields two or three kilometres outside Massa, where she had been born and grown up, and which, with a little girl to raise, she had had to leave for ever; the greasy, ruffled hair, the fat sensual lips, the lazy gestures of the only man in her life would become superimposed upon the figure of David, the young gentleman of Ferrara, Jewish, it's true, but belonging to one of the richest and most respected families of the town (those Camaiolis who lived on Corso Giovecca, just imagine, in that big house that they themselves owned), who for a long while had been making love to Lida, but whom she herself had never known, never once seen, even from a distance. She looked, she watched. Thin, sharp, whittled away by suffering and worry, it was as if in Lida she saw herself as a girl. Everything had been repeated, everything. From A to Z.

One evening she suddenly burst out laughing. She grabbed Lida by the hand and dragged her in front of the wardrobe mirror.

'Just look how similar we've become,' she said in a stifled voice.

And while nothing was audible in the room except the whisper of the carbide lamp, they remained staring at their faces for a long time, side by side, almost indistinguishable in the misted surface.

That's not to say that their relations always ran smoothly. Lida was not always prepared to listen without fighting back.

One evening, for example, Maria Mantovani had started telling her own story – something that could never have happened before. At the end she came out with a phrase that made Lida jump to her feet.

'If his parents had been in favour,' she had said, 'we'd have got married.'

Lying on the bed, her face hidden in her hands, Lida silently repeated these words, hearing once again the sigh full of resentment which had accompanied them. No, she wouldn't weep. And, to her mother, who had run after her and who had breathlessly leaned over her, she displayed, as she raised herself up, her cheeks dry, a look full of contempt and boredom.

Otherwise her irritations were rare and if they afflicted her, they did so without warning, like tempestuous squalls on a day of fine weather.

'Lida!' the daughter exclaimed once with a spiteful laugh (her mother was calling her by her name). 'How important it was for you when I went to the school that I wrote it on the exercise book with that flashy "y". What on earth did you think I was going to be – a showgirl?'

Maria Mantovani didn't reply. She smiled. Her daughter's tantrum transported her back to distant events, events whose significance she alone was in a position to assess. 'Lyda!' she kept repeating to herself. She thought about her own youth. She thought of Andrea, Andrea Tardozzi, the Massa Fiscaglia blacksmith who had been her sweetheart, her lover, and would have been her husband. She had come to live in the city with her baby, and every Sunday he travelled sixty kilometres by bicycle, thirty on the way there, and thirty back. He sat there, just where Lida was now sitting. She seemed to see him once again, with his leather jacket, his corduroy trousers, his tousled hair. Until one night, as he was returning to the village, he was taken by surprise by a heavy rain and fell ill with pleurisy. From then on she never saw him again. He had gone to live in Feltre in the Veneto: a small town at the foot of the mountains, where he took a wife and had children. If his parents hadn't been against it, and if, following that, he hadn't got ill, he would have married her. That was for sure. What did Lida know? What could she understand? She alone understood everything. For the two of them.

After supper, Lida was usually the first to go to bed. But the other bed, beside the one where she and the baby were already asleep, often remained untouched until late into the night, while in the centre of the table, still to be cleared, the gas lamp shed its blueish glow.

3.

Rather irregular in shape, its cobblestones partly overgrown with grass, Via Salinguerra is a small, subsidiary street which begins in an ill-shapen square, the result of an ancient demolition, and ends at the feet of the city's bastions quite close to Porta San Giorgio. This places it within the city and not that far from the medieval centre: to confirm this impression, you only need to look at the appearance of the houses which flank both its sides, all of them very poor and of modest proportions, and some old and decrepit, undoubtedly among the oldest in Ferrara. And yet, strolling down Via Salinguerra, even today, the kind of silence that surrounds it (heard from here, the city's church bells have a different timbre, as though muffled and lost) and especially the smell of manure, of ploughed earth, of cowsheds, which reveal the proximity of large hidden vegetable gardens, all contribute to the impression of already being outside the circle of the city walls, on the edge of the open countryside.

The restful voices of animals, of chickens, dogs, even oxen, distant bells, agricultural effluvia: sounds and smells even drifted down to the depths of the carpenter's storehouse where Lida and Maria Mantovani worked in men's tailoring. Seated just beside the window, almost as motionless and silent as the grey pieces of furniture behind them – as the table, that is, and the raffia armchairs, and the long narrow beds, the cradle, the wardrobe, the bedside table and three-legged washbowl with the ewer of water beside it, and further back, barely visible, the little door under the stairs which hid the small kitchen and toilet – when they raised their heads from the fabric, it was only to address the odd word to each other, to check that the baby didn't need anything, to look up outside at the rare passers-by, or, at the sudden shriek of the doorbell hung above the drab rectangle of the street door, to decide by a rapid exchange of glances which of the two would have to go upstairs to open it . . .

They passed three years like this.

And it might be supposed that many more would have passed in just the same manner, without any disruption or significant change, when life, which seemed to have forgotten them, suddenly recalled their existence through the person of a neighbour: a certain Benetti, Oreste Benetti, the owner of a bookbinding workshop in Via Salinguerra. The peculiar insistence with which he began to pay them visits in the evening after supper almost immediately assumed, at least for Maria, an unequivocal meaning. Yes – she thought, getting flustered – that Benetti's coming round expressly to see Lida . . . After all Lida was still young, very young indeed. At once she became lively, bustling, even happy. Without ever interrupting the talks between her daughter and the guest, she confined herself to walking about the room, glad to be there, it was clear, content to be present but self-contained, and to await and observe the emergence of a rare and delightful event.

In the meantime the one who spoke was nearly always was the bookbinder. About the years gone by: it seemed that he had no interest in any other topic.

'When Lida was a little girl' – he said – 'just this high', she often came to his workshop. She would enter, come forward, raise herself up on tiptoes so her eyes could be at the level of the workbench.

'Signor Benetti,' she would ask him in her little voice, 'would you give me a small piece of oiled paper?'

'Gladly,' he'd reply. 'But may I know what you want it for?'

'Nothing. Just to cover my exercise book.'

He would tell the story and laugh. Although he didn't speak to either of the women in particular, his looks were directed exclusively towards Lida. It was her attention and agreement that he sought. And while she observed the man in front of her (he had a very big head, which fitted his stout torso, but was out of proportion with the rest of his body), and in particular his large bony hands, forcibly clasped together on the tablecloth, she felt that at least in this respect she could hardly do other than try to please him. Facing him with a reserved courtesy, she spoke calmly, composedly and – deriving from this a strange, unaccustomed pleasure – in a somehow submissive manner.

Of nothing was the bookbinder more acutely aware than of his own importance. Nevertheless he was always in search of further kudos.

Once, on one of the few occasions when he addressed the old woman, even calling her by her Christian name, it was to remind her of the year she'd come to settle in Ferrara. Do you remember – he said – the cold we had that year? He did, very clearly. The abundant heaps of dirty snow that remained along both sides of the city streets until mid-April. And how the temperature had dropped so low the river Po itself had frozen.

'The Po itself!' he repeated with emphasis, widening his eyes.

It was as though he could still see it, he continued, the extraordinary sight of the river gripped in the sub-zero winds. Between the snow-heaped banks the river had ceased to flow, had totally seized up. So much so that, towards evening, instead of making use of the iron bridge at Pontelagoscuro to cross the river, some labourers – they must have been transporting firewood to a sawmill in Santa Maria Maddalena and were returning to Ferrara – preferred to risk their then-empty carts across the huge sheet of ice. What madmen! They advanced slowly, a few metres in front of their horses, holding the reins gathered in one fist behind their backs, as with their free hands they scattered sawdust, and meanwhile they whistled and yelled like the damned. Why were they whistling and yelling? Who knows? Perhaps to embolden the beasts, perhaps themselves. Or else simply to keep warm.

'I remember that famous winter,' he began one evening, with the respectful tone he always assumed when he spoke of people and things with any religious connection (orphaned as a child and brought up in a seminary, he had retained for the priests there, for priests as a whole, a filial reverence), 'I remember that famous winter, poor Don Castelli led us out every Saturday afternoon to Pontelagoscuro to look at the Po. As soon as we'd passed Porta San Benedetto the children broke out of their lines. Five kilometres there and five back – it wasn't just a stroll round the garden! And yet even to mention the tram to Don Castelli was big trouble. Although, given his age, he was gasping for air, he was always in front, always at the head of the whole troop with his fine soutane flowing and with yours truly at his side ... A veritable saint, sure enough, and a real father to my humble self!'

'I had just given birth to the baby,' Maria Mantovani put in, softly, in dialect, making the most of the silence that followed the bookbinder's speech. 'In town I felt lost,' she continued in Italian, 'I didn't really know anyone. But on the other hand how could I go back home? You know how it was, Oreste: in the country, it's mainly the mentality that's different.'

It seemed as though Oreste hadn't heard her.

'Apart from in 1917, there's never again been cold like that,' he reckoned, deep in thought. 'But what am I saying!' he added, raising his voice and shaking his head. 'It's not even comparable. In the winter of 1917 it was warm – on the Carso! You'd have to ask those on sick leave how it was here, those shirkers – whom we all know –' these final words he stressed with a sarcastic tone – 'never saw the Front, not even on a postcard.'

Taking in the unusually brutal dig directed at Andrea Tardozzi, the blacksmith at Massa Fiscaglia who had been let off service because of pleurisy and for that reason hadn't been sent to war (in 1910 he had moved to Feltre, the Feltre up near the Alps, where he had settled with his family), Maria Mantovani stiffened, offended. And for the rest of that evening, cast out to brood alone in her corner over the innumerable events in her life that might have happened and that didn't, she spoke not another word.

As far as the bookbinder was concerned, having established, as he felt impelled to, the proper distance between them, he briskly resumed all the courtesy and gallantry that was his by nature. It was usually on himself and his own past that he dwelled. Till he was twenty, twenty-five, all had gone badly – he sighed – from every point of view. But afterwards, work had changed that, his work, *his* craft, and from then on things turned around completely. 'We craftsmen,' he used to say, with no lack of pride, looking Lida straight in the eyes. Never distracted, Lida quietly received his gaze. And he was grateful, one could see it, that she always sat there, on the other side of the table, so silently, so serenely, so attentively, thereby corresponding in her whole aspect to his secret ideal of womanhood.

The bookbinder often talked on till midnight. Having exhausted his store of personal anecdotes, he began to talk of religion, of history, of the economy and so on, lapsing into frequent, bitter observations – expressed of course in a low tone – about the anti-Catholic politics of the Fascists. During the first period of his visits, without ceasing to listen to him, Lida would use the tip of her toe to rock the cradle in which Ireneo slept until he was four years old. Later, when he had grown a bit and had a little bed of his own (he grew up slight and frail, having contracted a long infectious illness when he was five that, apart from permanently weakening his health, undoubtedly influenced the frailty and lack of conviction of his character), Lida would get up from her chair every now and then and, approaching the child who was asleep, would lean over and place a hand on his forehead.

4.

In the summer of 1928, Lida had her twenty-fifth birthday.

One evening, while she and Oreste Benetti sat in their usual places, divided as ever by the table and the lamp, suddenly, very simply, the bookbinder asked her if she would marry him.

Soberly, without showing the least surprise, Lida stared at him.

It was as if she were seeing him for the first time. She considered with extraordinary care every detail of his face, his very black, watery eyes, his tall, white forehead topped by an arch of iron-grey hair cut short, like a toothbrush, in the style of certain priests and soldiers, and she was astounded to find herself there, to be taking note of all this only now, so late. He must have been about fifty. At least.

She was suddenly stricken by a wave of anxiety. Not able to say anything, she turned in search of help towards her mother, who, having risen to her feet, had come to the table and was leaning on it with both her hands. The grimace of impending tears that was already pulling down the corners of her mouth only added to her confusion.

'What's wrong with you?' she shouted angrily at her daughter in dialect. 'Would you say what's wrong?'

Lida rose abruptly to her feet, rushed towards, then up the stairs – she left, slamming the door, and went down the other staircase to the entrance.

Having finally reached the street, she immediately leant her back against the wall beside the dark gaping cavity of the wide-open doorway, and looked at the sky.

It was a magnificent starscape. In the distance a band could be heard. Where were they playing? she asked herself, with a sudden, spasmodic desire to mingle with the crowd, happy, dressed in a pinafore and holding an ice-cream in her hand like a young girl without a care in the world. Was the sound coming from San Giorgio, in the clearing beside the church? Or else from Porta Reno, perhaps the Piazza Travaglio itself?

But by then her breathing was no longer so laboured. And there it was, coming through the walls of old brick against which she rested the whole of her spine, there it was, reaching her, the whispering voice of Oreste Benetti. He was speaking to her mother, now, quietly as though nothing had happened. What was he saying? Who could tell? Whatever the words, his voice, the placid, subdued hum of his voice was enough to persuade her to calm down, to encourage her to go back inside. When she reappeared at the stair landing she was once again mistress of herself, of her thoughts and her gestures.

Having shut the door, gone down the stairs neither too hurriedly nor too deliberately, taking care not to catch the eyes of either the bookbinder or her mother – during her absence the two of them had remained in their places, he seated at the table, she standing: and there they still were, silent, examining her face with inquisitive gazes. She passed close by the table, sat down again in her place, and almost imperceptibly narrowed her shoulders. And the topic of marriage – for the nearly two hours that their guest still remained – was not broached again, nor was it in the course of the innumerable other evenings that were to follow.

This doesn't mean to suggest that Oreste Benetti nurtured any doubt whatsoever about what Lida's response would sooner or later be. Quite the contrary. For him, from the first moment after this, it was as though Lida had already consented, as though they were already fiancés.

This was evident from the different way he treated her: always solicitous and kind, yes, but within, deep down, there was an air of authority which had been lacking before. At this juncture, he alone – it seemed as though he wanted to declare – was in a position to guide her through life.

In his view, Lida's character had a serious defect – he was willing to say it openly, in such cases, not hesitating to call on Maria Mantovani as a witness with a sideways glance – which was always to be looking backwards, always to be chewing over the past. Why not, for a change, force herself to look a little the other way, towards the future? Pride was a great ugly beast. Like a snake, it slithered in where you least expected it.

'You need to be reasonable,' he sighed by way of conclusion. 'You need to stay calm and keep going forwards.'

Other times, however, in apparent self-contradiction, it was actually he – even if by nods, by hints and carefully veiled insinuations, with Lida following the skilful, tireless workings of his mind without ever reacting, as though hypnotized – it was actually he who showed her the picture of her youth: unregulated, anarchic, unaware of the urgent need to achieve a higher maturity, a dignified and tranquil way of life.

And on this topic, yes, certainly – he also let it be understood – since he loved her, he naturally understood, made excuses for her, forgave *everything*. His feelings, however, were not so blinded, she should realize, as to stop him remembering (and making her remember) that she had committed a gross error, a mortal sin from which she would only be absolved the day she was married. What on earth had she imagined? Had she perhaps dreamed that a man of her own breed, who, besides, as she was well aware, was almost thirty years older, could think of love outside of marriage, of a Catholic marriage? This was a duty, a mission. The true believer was incapable of conceiving of life, and consequently of the relationship between man and woman, in any other way . . .

All three of them, however, were in such a state of nervous tension, were so continually on the alert, that it would have needed little indeed to throw the fragile balance of their relations into crisis. After every clash, they remained uneasy, sulky, holding on to their grudges.

On one occasion, for example, referring to Ireneo, the bookbinder said that truly he wished the baby well: just as if he were his father. Betrayed by the heat of the moment, he had let himself go a shade too far.

'But just a second, aren't you *Uncle* Oreste?' exclaimed Ireneo, who was already seven years old, and had acquired the habit of showing him his homework before he was put to bed.

'Of course . . . you understand . . . It was only a manner of speaking. What strange things go through your mind!'

The bookbinder's confusion suddenly gave Lida a precise sense of her own importance. While, a bit breathlessly, the good man kept on talking to the child, she and her mother exchanged glances and smiled.

But the moments of silent tension and malice were, all considered, quite rare. To avert them, or leave them behind, presents always played a useful role. Right from the start, Oreste Benetti had always been lavish with those. Although he had made it clear that after the wedding they would all move together to a little villa beyond Porta San Benedetto (for which he was already negotiating terms of sale with a building firm, but, despite that, he had promptly had the electric lights installed and the walls whitewashed and had bought various bits of furniture, a cheap cast-iron stove, a picture, various kitchen utensils, a couple of flower vases and so on), it was as if the marriage, about which, it was evident, he never for a moment stopped thinking, were something he hadn't the slightest intention of rushing. He was in love – he said so with his presents – which were often useless, it's true, and sometimes a bit absurd. If he married her, it was because he loved her. He had never in his life been engaged before, not even once. Neither as a youth nor later as a man had he ever tasted the inebriating pleasure of giving presents to a fiancée. Now that this pleasure was allowed him, he had every right to see that things proceeded slowly, gradually, with a rigorous respect for all the rules.

He came round every evening at the same time: at nine-thirty on the dot.

Lida would hear him coming from afar, from as far as the street.

And there it was, the vigorous ringing of the bell that announced him, and there were his steady footsteps on the staircase, on the entrance side, and up there, at the level of the landing, his cheerful greeting.

'Good evening, ladies!'

He would begin to descend, still humming that air from *The Barber of Seville* between his teeth, then interrupt himself halfway down the stairs with a polite cough. And suddenly the room would be full of him, of the little man who wore his hair a bit like a soldier, a bit like a priest, and of his heated, brisk and imperious presence.

His arrival scene was always the same – for years it never changed. Although she could predict it in every particular, each time Lida was overcome by a kind of lulled stupefaction.

She would let him come forward, without even giving him a nod or getting to her feet.

But *before*, how had it been then in those cherished days?

Oh, at that time, when an equally vigorous ringing signalled that David, wrapped in his hefty blue coat with the fur collar, stamping his feet on the cobblestones out of impatience and the cold, was waiting for her, as agreed, outside the front entrance on the street – he had never wanted to come in, never felt the need to be introduced! – then, on the contrary, she'd had very little time to grab her overcoat from the wardrobe, put it on, shut the wardrobe and bring her face up to the mirror on the wall, furiously dab some powder on and adjust her hair. She was only conceded those few, precious seconds. And yet they were more than enough, as in the large mirror, looking small and shiny, with her hair drawn back behind her head (the light behind her made her seem almost bald), she saw the grey head of her mother appear and disappear, rapid and darting behind her back.

'What are you gawping at?' she turned to shout at her. 'D'you know what? I've had enough – enough of you and this whole life.'

She went out, slamming the door. David didn't like to be kept waiting.

5.

Still trembling, grasping his arm, she would let herself be led away.

Rather than turning right and heading towards the city centre, they usually went down Via Salinguerra until they reached the bastions, and then from there, walking at a good pace along the path that topped the city walls, they would arrive at Porta Reno in about twenty minutes. It was David's preference. Since he had made peace with his family – so as to free himself later, he said, when he was in a better position to do so, but in the meantime he would graduate, he really needed to graduate! – it was worth their being careful for now, at least to avoid being seen around together. At this point, it was indispensable, he kept on repeating. Given the situation, she herself ought to be convinced that certain 'ostentatious shows' ought to be well and truly done with. By 'ostentatious shows' he was referring to the earliest period of their relationship, when, throwing down a gauntlet, he was even willing to take her to the Salvini cinema in the evenings, when they would go to sit in the main caffès, including the Borsa, in daylight, and he'd proclaim that he'd already had more than enough of the boring and hypocritical life he'd been leading up till now – university, friends, family and so on. Anyway, wasn't it much better this way? he would hurriedly add, with a grin. Aren't hindrances, subterfuges, the best spur and incentive for love? In any case, one fact was for sure: along that path on top of the walls, or, soon after, at the little cinema in Piazza Travaglio where they were heading, no one from his family or 'circle' would ever encounter them.

Regardless of all that, she kept up alongside him in silence, frozen in body and soul.

And yet, after a little while, almost as soon as she found herself in the crowded, smoky stalls of the Diana, seated next to David with her eyes fixed on the screen, her frayed nerves quickly relaxed. Not seldom the films narrated love stories in which, despite everything, she kept dreaming of herself as the heroine: something that in the final moments induced her not only to look round at David (in the penumbra cut in mid-air by the elongated, blue cone of light which sprang from the projector behind, she could discern his long, thin neck, with his large, protruding Adam's apple just above the tie-knot, his unhappy profile, always seeming to be drowsy, his brown, brilliantined hair slightly curly at the temples), but also to seek out his hand and grasp it anxiously. And David? Ready as he was to return her look and give an answering squeeze to her hand, he seemed relaxed, even to be in a good mood. But she could never rely on that. After having let her hold his hand for a while, he would sometimes withdraw it brusquely. He would move his whole body away, or else, if he hadn't already taken off his coat, he would stand up and do so. 'It's so hot in here,' he'd sigh heavily, 'you can hardly breathe.'

Intimidated, she would make no further attempt at closeness. She would quickly return her gaze to the screen, and from then on David would be down there, in the middle of the large grey luminescent rectangle that filled the end of the auditorium, intent on lighting a cigarette with his gloved hands, dancing in his dinner jacket, or staring into the eyes of stunningly beautiful women, pressing himself against their breasts, kissing them lingeringly on the mouth . . . The film so entranced her that later, when it was over, and she was outside again, if David slipped an arm under hers and speaking in caressing tones, offered to accompany her home the same way they'd come, she would violently start awake, as from a kind of sleep.

'It's only a little longer, that way,' David would urge her.

'But it's late, my mother was expecting me back at midnight,' she tried to reply. 'And then the cold, it'll be all wet . . .'

How much better it would be, she thought in the meantime, to return home by cutting back through the centre of town! With the mist that had descended – in those two hours it had become so dense that the yellow lights of the streetlamps could barely be seen – no one, they could be sure, would have noticed them, not even if they'd passed by the Listone caffè, or if they'd taken the Corso Giovecca. They could have slowly walked along the pavements slippery with the damp, their lips and eyelashes laden with the tepid droplets, holding each other tightly like two real, proper fiancés, and talking, God – or rather David – willing. What would he have talked about? Perhaps the film (what a ham the main actor was! – he would have said – and also the star, what a silly thing she was!), or perhaps about himself, his studies, his plans for the future . . . Finally, before parting, they might even have been able to slip into some small caffè, one of those in the Saraceno district or in Via Borgo di Sotto. Seating them both in a corner, David would then have ordered two small drinks. After which, in the warmth, sipping the aniseed and thinking of going to bed soon and to sleep, she could have felt, have been infused with, if not happiness, at least a sense of being in tune with herself and with life.

But instead she would give in.

And they would quickly make their way towards the city walls, away from the bicycle bells of the local lads who would hang around the cinema's still wide-open glass doors, talking in loud voices about sport or who knows what, or else eating roast chestnuts bought for a few *centesimi* from the old woman with the black shawl, the woollen half-gloves, the grey overcoat, forever stooped there over her little cast-iron griddle, they would be cat-calling to her with whistles, shouts, disrespectful hisses and swearwords. It was no use hurrying past. The ever-growing distance seemed to render the cries even more acute and penetrating. They followed her closely. Like cold, clammy hands which tried to grasp her, to touch her under her clothes.

With the first darkness, in the first field they came to, she was pushed down on to the grass. With her chin on his shoulder, without closing her eyes, she let him do what he wanted.

Later, she would be the first to get up. And if, at a certain point, she felt the desire to struggle beneath him, to bite him, do him harm (David never resisted this: instead, relaxing his long back, he would lean on her with his whole weight), that was when her rage, the sort of anger which lately had induced her to push him off her, would suddenly give way to a tremendous feeling of anxiety, of fear. How far away he already was! she thought, while she strained to get up, to smooth down her dress. Nothing at all mattered to him, now! And yet, why consider him the guilty party? Hadn't she herself been perfectly able to imagine how the evening would end? From when they met, in front of the street entrance, hardly exchanging a greeting, from when they had hurriedly walked towards the city walls, everything had been utterly predictable.

They went on their way.

She was fully aware of all this. He was cold and distracted. Nothing he could say now would do anything but wound her. And yet she would provoke him.

For example, she would ask him: 'What's your mother's name again?'

As David kept silent, she would reply on his behalf, with slow emphasis: 'Teresa.'

Wasn't it funny that she'd ask such pointless questions, and then that it should be her replying, stressing each syllable like a schoolgirl being tested?

'And Marina,' she continued, 'what is your sister Marina called?'

She burst out laughing, then repeated: 'Ma-ri-na.'

Hastening his steps over the frost-hardened ground, David yawned. But he finally decided to speak.

What he uttered was strange and muffled. There was without doubt some truth in it, but also – and it sufficed to listen carefully to his tone, to realize this – a great deal of fiction. He spoke in general about himself, and especially about his 'romantic involvement' with a young lady of the highest society, about whom, without disclosing her name, he kept on boasting, not just about her beauty, but also her urbane manners, her aristocratic and refined tastes. Their meetings, their tiffs (since, it seemed, they often quarrelled) always occurred in the midst of glittering occasions: a charity ball at the Union Club, that would have been attended by the nobility, a gala showing at the City Theatre, a gallop in the country which ended in a spectacular gathering at some beautiful villa encircled by a vast park. All things considered, it was 'a far from smooth relationship', hindered by both families, certainly, but 'solely' due to their different religions: a relationship in whose context the 'thing' that they had just done, in the field, would never, even by mistake, be mentioned

Within the Walls

... In the meantime, they had come down from the bastions, and entered Via Salinguerra. And if, till that moment she had been listening in silence, almost holding her breath, as soon as she gathered, from the shapes of the houses and the streetlamps, that in a few moments they would have to part, this caused her to suffer a nervous agitation of such intensity as to make her fear she might lose all control. Oh, how she hated, at that moment, her miserable, worn-out coat, her ruffled hair, flattened at the temples by the damp, her common-looking hands, deformed by work and frost! But what could she do then but try to keep calm? Small of stature, without the least attraction, of physique or personality (if only she'd played the tart a bit more!), she might as well accept her fate now, since it had already been sealed. Who knows? If at that point she'd been able to keep her composure, perhaps David would have been grateful to her. Perhaps in the future he'd have been able to treat her like an old friend to whom every request is conceded, who'd be able to give him any advice, even the most unwelcome. Not much to ask? Little enough. Still, better than nothing.

By then they'd have gone through the gate and reached the entrance.

Though his voice was reduced to a whisper, David kept on talking. What was he saying?

Soon after he graduated – he might, for example, be saying – he would get the hell out, not only of Ferrara, but of Italy. He was fed up with the tedious life of the provinces, of rotting in this hole of a city. Almost certainly he would be off to America, to stay there and settle, definitively.

With whom would he go to America? she had risked asking him on one occasion. Alone, or with that young lady he liked so much?

'Alone,' he'd replied, annoyed.

He wasn't the type to marry, he'd added. Anyone. As things were now, all he wanted was a change of air, he'd already told her. Nothing more than that.

She had said nothing in reply. She'd merely nodded in the dark.

Another time though – and she would regret it later, in bed, when the ticking of the alarm clock on the bedside table and the wheezing noise her mother made while sleeping had kept her awake – she had burst out laughing.

She had asked him: 'And if I got pregnant?'

She was well aware that a question of this kind would succeed in detaining David for another five minutes. What he would say in those five minutes didn't matter to her. What mattered was that before going he would feel obliged to kiss her.

6.

The winter of 1929 was unusually hard. To find another to compare to it, Oreste Benetti declared, you'd have to go back as far as the famous winter of 1903, when even the river Po was frozen over, or perhaps to the winter of 1917.

It began to snow before Christmas, and it kept snowing until the eve of Epiphany. Yet the cold was still a long way from the extraordinary levels it would reach in the following months. There was even, just after Epiphany, a brief interlude of sun, almost spring-like in its warmth, and the snow had already begun to melt.

'Can it be trusted?' Maria Mantovani wondered.

From the bed, where since around the start of December she had been confined because of a feverish flu, which had left her face lined and her chest racked by an ugly cough, the old woman listened to the splashing and squelching from the occasional vehicle that passed along Via Salinguerra. No, it couldn't be trusted, she ended by replying to herself, the corners of her mouth turned down in a bitter grimace. That spell of warmth, but rather than warmth all that mist which from the early afternoon onwards swept in from the surrounding countryside and seemed to drench everything just as if it were rain, didn't help at all in fostering any illusions.

Then, as soon as he came in (he now came in without ringing the bell, as Lida had given him a key some time ago), Oreste Benetti divested himself of his sodden greatcoat, hung it on a nail sticking out of the entrance door. He came down the stairs, happy as can be.

At length, after seating himself, as ever, at the head of the table, he began to talk.

For a couple of months, that is, since Ireneo had started going to the seminary, the main topic of his speeches had been the boy himself. Naturally, he was saying, there was no point in rushing to decide. All the same, in his modest opinion, from now on it was worth considering what job Ireneo would do when he was grown-up. The first three years at junior high school – those in any case he ought to do. But afterwards? Take him out of school and put him immediately to work somewhere? No – they agreed that wasn't an option. And yet once he'd got his certificate from middle school, a choice regarding the various schools (at Ferrara it wasn't as if there was only the high school, no, there were the Training Colleges, the Technical Institute from which one graduated as an accountant or surveyor, not to mention the Industrial Institute in the Vicolo Mozzo Roversella!), a choice of one kind or another couldn't be avoided.

One evening, on his arrival, not without solemnity, he announced that that very afternoon he had dropped in at the seminary. He was invited in by Don Bonora, the director, who had taken over some twenty years ago from poor Don Castelli, and he had asked him about Ireneo.

'What can I say?' Don Bonora had at first somewhat guardedly replied. 'We are just starting out on logical analysis and grammar. We have yet to begin a real study of Latin . . .'

He had then tried to sound out the director on what he thought of Ireneo's character. To which, the priest, although continuing to express himself with great prudence and tact, had replied that yes, effectively, the boy's character gave him some cause for concern. It was too early, you understand, he had added, to formulate any definitive judgement of him . . . but that we were dealing with a slightly weak, distracted character, of this, unfortunately, there seemed to him little doubt.

The bookbinder compressed his lips. Then, all of a sudden, he began to talk of the weather.

'In my opinion, we're not clear of it,' he declared, raising his eyes to the ceiling and sniffing the air cautiously, 'the worst is yet to come.'

And Maria Mantovani, stretched out on her bed at the end of the room (from the table where the bookbinder and Lida usually sat facing each other, one could see nothing but her pallid prominent nose, with the two black vertical holes of her nostrils), immediately nodded in agreement, smiling in silence at some private thought.

Oreste Benetti was right. The worst of the winter was yet to come. At the start of the last third of January, as it happened, the sky once again became overcast, the temperature dropped, and as vicious gusts disturbed the air, it began to snow again with a furious intensity. It was like being high up in the mountains. Reduced to mere pathways, or narrow tracks arduously kept clear by the teams of shovellers the town council had hurriedly employed, the streets, especially the smaller ones, provided thoroughfare only for pedestrians. Since, from the outset, many of the city's bastions had become the destination for enthusiastic crowds of impromptu skiers, mainly students, at a given point it was decided by the Fascist Federation, to promote competitions up there, and especially along that stretch of the walls that runs between Porta San Giorgio and Porta Reno. This meant that Via Salinguerra, usually so deserted and silent, became transformed from one day to the next into a gathering place of much noise and bustle.

Quite suddenly Maria Mantovani's health worsened. Her fever began to run high; she became breathless. A doctor was called, and after a rapid examination, he announced that she was suffering from pneumonia. Was she in danger? Without doubt she was!, the doctor confirmed, in reply to the direct question addressed to him by the little man of advanced years, perhaps a relative, who had called him out. The general condition of the patient which, even at a cursory glance, looked precarious, hardly promised a happy outcome.

Predicted and feared, the crisis came on the fifth day following.

Maria Mantovani didn't take her eyes off the window. Beyond the glass, which the daylight struggled to filter through, she could make out the snow falling thickly, in scurries. She seemed to be struggling to hear. Via Salinguerra resounded feebly with happy cries

Within the Walls

and hurrying footsteps. What was going on out there? she wondered. It was as if the city were having a celebration. But how come every voice, every sound, seemed to reach her from so far away?

'I can't hear clearly,' she complained. 'I can't hear any more. It's as if my ears have been stuffed with cotton wool.'

'It's snowing,' Lida replied softly, sitting at the bedside. 'That's why it all sounds so muffled to you.'

The old woman gave a knowing little laugh.

'It's not as though it's *because of that*,' she murmured, shaking her head and lowering her eyelids.

After a couple of hours her wheezing became a death rattle. A priest ought to be called. And the bookbinder, who had suddenly vanished, in fact quickly returned with the parish priest of Santa Maria in Vado.

In the meantime the room had filled with people.

They were mainly the women of the neighbourhood who, although no one had alerted them, spontaneously appeared. How had they got in? Lida found herself wondering. Was it possible that Oreste (Oreste, heavens – she noticed herself calling him simply by his first name, which she had never done before . . .), was it possible that Oreste had forgotten to shut the front door behind him? However it had happened, a half-hour later, when the priest had gone away, the neighbours didn't leave the room. They all stayed: huddled underneath the window with their shawls over their heads and fervently whispering.

Rigid in the centre of the room, Oreste Benetti held his hands together.

As soon as the death rattle ceased he came forwards and leant over the sickbed. Lightly and precisely, his hands moved to close the half-open eyes of Maria Mantovani, to cross her skeletal arms over her chest, and then, with a final, dextrous touch, to smooth the rumpled sheet and reposition the coverlet which had slipped almost entirely on to the floor.

All this time, until the bookbinder, having finished his work, was on the point of leaving soundlessly, Lida hadn't made a single movement. But even after those big busy hands had withdrawn, hands that belonged to the man who, soon enough, she knew it as a certainty by now, would become her husband, even afterwards, she stayed there seated beside the bed, to stare at the waxen profile of her mother. Her almost closed eyelids, her nose that suddenly appeared too big, too prominent, her lips hinting at a vague, absurdly happy smile: the whole, all-too-familiar physiognomy revealed itself as different at a stroke, so much so that it was as if only then was she able to perceive it in all its particularity. As if she could keep on and on staring at her mother's face. While she did so, she felt something old, something bitter, something hard slowly dissolving within her.

She covered her face with her hands and began to weep silently.

Finally she raised her head, turning her eyes full of tears towards the bookbinder.

'Leave me be,' she said in a low voice. 'You too, Oreste,' she added, nodding, 'go away as well.'

'Quite, quite, my dear . . .' he stammered, intimidated.

The neighbourhood women were already leaving. After he'd tagged along behind their group halfway up the stairs, Oreste was the last to reach the landing and, closing the door, the last to disappear.

With her elbow resting on the sickbed and her cheek on her palm, Lida, left alone, thought about her mother, about herself, about their two lives. But she was mainly thinking of David, and the room in the big apartment block on Via Mortara where, at the beginning of that distant spring, she had gone to live with him.

It had happened like this.

One evening, at the end of winter – that same winter during which, because of the boredom and irritability which showed in David's every word and gesture, she was expecting any moment for him to say to her, 'That's enough, Lida, from now on it would be better if we stopped seeing each other', and she was eaten away by this waiting – an evening just like many others, David had suggested to her out of the blue that they 'set up house together like any normal working-class couple' in the big apartment block on Via Mortara. He had decided to make a clean break with his family, he had added, in order to 'forge a new life for himself'. He was prepared to live in a 'garret', a 'fine, poetic garret under the eaves', with a view not only of the whole city, but also 'of the countryside as far as the hills of Bologna'. In order 'to support his family' he'd be willing 'to work in the sugar factory' . . . And she? What else could she do apart from immediately assenting, as she had on that other occasion, the first, when, meeting him by chance in the open-air locale of Borgo San Giorgio (she being at that time little more than sixteen, in every way a mere girl) they had remained together as a couple for the whole evening, and then, towards midnight, ended up in a field close by the city walls? Yet again, she hadn't asked herself a thing, hadn't hesitated for a single moment. A few evenings later, she had left the house with a bundle under her arms which her mother, as usual, hadn't dared to comment on, though had surely noticed. Just like that: Goodbye! What madness! And yet, only later, much later, after having given birth, when she had returned to stay alone in the room at the big apartment block, and the child wouldn't stop crying, and she sensed her breasts every day were producing less and less milk, and she had hardly any *lire* left, only then did she begin to rouse herself from the long waking dream that her life had been until then.

But David, who was he? she now asked herself after many years. What was he looking for, what did he really want?

In the big apartment block, in a room on the floor below, lived the family of a nurse at the Sant'Anna Hospital. They were called Mastellari, and there were six of them: the nurse, his wife and four children.

Mornings when she went down with the pitcher to bring water from the courtyard, it wasn't unusual for her to bump into Signora Mastellari.

'What does your husband do?' the woman had once asked her. 'Does he work in a factory?'

'Yes – but at the moment he's unemployed. Soon he'll be working in the sugar factory,' she had replied calmly, utterly sure that David, a student, the son of well-to-do parents, and quite regardless of whether he was late with his graduation and had broken with his family, would never in a million years end up working in that factory.

A factory worker – just imagine it! And yet what was it that David most aspired to be if not a 'typical worker'. Wasn't that what he kept on repeating?

It was enough that he talked, and then everything became simple, easy, attainable. To get married? He had always considered marriage a joke – he would declare once again – one of the most typical and nauseating 'bourgeois idiocies'. But seeing that she was at heart drawn to 'nuptials', he would quickly add, smiling, that she shouldn't fret, at the most within a year, when he'd found work – 'a position at the town hall' – he would undoubtedly be able to make a respectable woman of her. It was certain. He would marry her; he had no hesitation in promising her that. Confronted with her 'more than legitimate and comprehensible aspiration' to become his wife, his 'wife also as regards the law', not only did he not draw back, but rather he would have done his utmost so that 'the time all this would take' should be speeded up . . .

The afternoons, those sweltering summer afternoons, he generally passed stretched out, nearly always asleep. His breathing was so slow, his cheeks so pallid under a few days' growth of beard, that at times she – seated beside his bed exactly as she now was beside her mother's bed – couldn't resist the temptation to take him by the arm and give him a shake. 'What is it?' he'd grumble, seemingly unable to lift his eyelids. Then, turning towards the wall – his pyjama top from behind was soaked with sweat – he would fall back into a deep sleep.

Usually, as soon as they'd had their supper, they went out. In search of coolness, they'd adopted the habit of staying out late at Porta Mare. That rather crowded kilometre which separated the big apartment block from Porta Mare was worth putting up with. A little further on from the Customs barrier, there was an ice-cream kiosk with ten or so small tables in front, and ice-cream, as David knew, she'd always loved since she was a baby.

Taking Via Fossato di Mortara, you came to the city walls in a few moments. And it had been up there, on one of those evenings, that she had suddenly stopped walking.

'Listen. I think I'm going to have a child,' she said very calmly, putting her hand on David's arm.

At that moment, he didn't seemed surprised. Not a gesture from him, not a word.

A little later, though, after they'd reached the usual kiosk, and she stood there with her chest leaning on the edge of the zinc counter and her eyes dazzled by the light of the acetylene lamp, he gently asked her:

'And what would you like? Lemon or chocolate?'

Without showing any desire to sit down, he had already begun to lick his ice-cream (as ever a custard-and-vanilla combination). But he seemed sad, disappointed. While he licked his ice-cream, he looked at her; he examined her from head to toe.

'The heat's unbearable this evening,' he'd exclaimed at a certain point, puffing. 'To think that, up in the mountains as soon as it gets dark, you have to put on a pullover.'

He was evidently referring to his family, who from the first of June had been holidaying up in Cortina d'Ampezzo.

'Where have they gone to stay, your family?' she'd found the strength to ask (as she too began licking her ice-cream, having once again chosen a chocolate one). 'Have they rented a house?'

'No. They've gone to the Miramonti. Imagine a kind of castle –' he seemed eager to explain – 'with a wood all round it, six or seven times the size of the Finzi-Contini garden, that one down there at Piopponi, you know, by the Mura degli Angeli, and at least a dozen times bigger than Montagnone . . .'

Who was David? What was he looking for? What did he want? And why?

To these questions there was no reply, and there never would be. Besides, it was late. Someone, most likely Oreste, was knocking on the window. She needed to get up, force herself up to the street door and tell him he could come back inside.

7.

It was indeed Oreste.

After having caught up with the neighbours down at the entrance, for a good half-hour Oreste had stayed to talk to the women of what had happened and chiefly to listen to them. But then the cluster had moved on into the street and dispersed, and he, left alone, had begun to walk up and down in front of the doorway.

He felt two opposite emotions colliding within him, two conflicting necessities.

On the one hand, he felt the pressing need to rush off and lock up his workshop, so as to be able to confront with the required diligence all that the death of Maria Mantovani saddled him with. And yet the thought of Lida held him back. Several times, bending down and bringing his face close to the steamed-up windowpane, he had tried to peer into the room. Down there, next to the bed, on the right-hand side, he made out a small, curved, motionless, grey figure.

'What's she up to?' he grumbled after a while, with the affectionate impatience of someone who already considered himself a husband.

The first shadows of evening were falling. It had stopped snowing, but it was still bitterly cold. Through the windows of houses round about could be glimpsed the insides of kitchens, cramped, illuminated dining-rooms. He should get a move on and bring things to a head. At last, having yet again bent down to peer into the window (too dark – he concluded: by now he could make out nothing at all), he decided to tap on the window. He stood there, listening, his heart beating dully in his chest, until he seemed to hear Lida's footsteps ascending the staircase inside. In response he was quick to slip through the entrance. A second before she lowered the handle and opened the door, he was already on the landing.

Straight away, at first glance, he was aware that he once again had the upper hand. Her back leaning against the doorframe, and her eyes seeming to surrender themselves to his own, Lida stared at him in silence. That he should protect her: in her whole demeanour there was no other request.

'Good Lord, you really oughtn't to spend the night like this!' he said with lowered voice, in dialect, almost roughly.

Then, still whispering, without crossing the threshold, he began to explain to her what he meant to do.

He had to rush off and close the workshop, and since after that he also had to sort out another small matter, he wouldn't be able to get back for at least a couple of hours. Before going to the workshop, though, he would stop for a minute at the house of one of the neighbours, Signora Bedini. As she had offered to give a hand, he'd ask her to come round.

'Why?' he exclaimed, forestalling a possible objection on Lida's part. 'Goodness me, to keep you company . . . to make you a bit of supper . . . Or even just to pray with you!'

At the word 'supper' Lida had shaken her head as a sign of refusal. But the argument that had followed was stronger than her resistance. She lowered her eyes, and he looked at her with a smile.

'So that's agreed then,' he warned, 'don't put the door chain on. Better still, leave the door ajar. D'you understand?'

And squeezing her hand, he disappeared up the stairs.

The temperature fell sharply during the night. The thin pinkish light which the following morning tried to pierce through the ice-encrusted windows – Lida was stretched out on her bed, Signora Bedini was curled in an armchair while Oreste, who had spent long stretches of the night in prayer, was on his feet at the window scrutinizing the weather – the light seemed to have arrived from a faraway sun, lost in the vague and misty blue of the sky, a sun that gave no warmth.

Just at that moment – Oreste calculated, with his coat collar raised over the stubbly thick silver hairs on the back of his neck while he blew on his frozen fingers – just at that moment the thermometer must be showing way below zero: ten, fifteen, twenty, who could say? That, however, should have made the weather more stable. During January, and perhaps up till mid February, the cold might drop to an even lower level: so that when the canals in the countryside, the river Reno and even the Po, had frozen over, the pipes of drinking water burst, and so on, in the end the winter would be comparable only with that of 1903. Would the farm produce suffer? Perhaps not. He at any rate felt rather sanguine (and felt not the least bit of embarrassment in admitting it), glad to have figured everything out exactly.

Maria Mantovani's funeral took place late afternoon that same day.

The third-class carriage advanced, unhindered, over the flattened snow, and behind, apart from the priest and a small cleric, Oreste walked alone. Submitting to his advice, Lida had remained at home. As for him, the old schoolboy of the seminary, the favourite of Don Castelli, the veteran of the Carso front, all the extremes of the weather imbued him with energy, restored to him as if by magic the missed hours of sleep from the night before. He walked with lowered gaze. With a pace that he instinctively accorded with that of the priest, he unceasingly studied the grooves cut into the snow by the carriage's tall thin wheels, the little slippages of snow that, detaching themselves from the wheel rims, barely powdered the shiny black varnish of the spokes and the leaf springs.

When he got back it was already night. And from the street, rather than knocking on the window-panes as he had in the past few days, he wanted to announce himself with the emphatic ring of the bell that was his trademark.

Lida was awaiting him at the bottom of the stairs. She must have been asleep. And yet her face, before marked with the signs of weariness, now seemed refreshed and rested. She was completely transformed.

He sat down in his accustomed seat, leaning his folded arms on the table, and looking over at Lida, who was keeping herself busy about the cheap stove. He didn't miss a single gesture. He observed her with a most particular expression, a mixture of joy and gratitude, which surfaced in his eyes every time he thought he could discern in any phrase or gesture or even in a simple look of hers the attempt or desire to please him.

'Tonight it would best to call on Signora Bedini again,' he said after a while. 'I'll stop by at hers later. Tomorrow I'm thinking of paying a visit to Don Bonora. I think that for the next couple of weeks the boy should sleep round at his house. And then we shall see.'

Already it was he who decided, who chose what would happen in the future.

After supper, away from the table that still had to be cleared, they remained there to discuss things. Limiting himself to Maria Mantovani and her life, Oreste spoke at length and with much tenderness. He remarked that she had suffered a great deal in her lifetime, poor thing, because she had loved very much, because she had had too much heart. He then described the plot in the Municipal Cemetery where tomorrow morning she would be laid to rest.

It was a really lovely place, he assured her, very respectable. Had she not seen it yet, the recently constructed arcade added to the right side of the San Cristoforo Church, making a great symmetrical curve identical to the arcade next to Via Borso, which had been built also to complete the colonnade in front of Certosa, on the Mura degli Angeli side? Well, her mother would be buried there, under those new arches. No, no – he confirmed – at midday, with the sun that would shine there from dawn to dusk, as in a greenhouse, the spot was really splendid.

'It's true that those places there, on that side,' he added after a pause, and tightening his lips, 'will cost a tidy packet.'

But immediately, fearing that he might have been misunderstood, he explained that God forbid, she, Lida, shouldn't worry in any way about the expense.

'After working for so many years,' he exclaimed, 'thank heavens I've been able to save up a little something!'

And since she, he continued, without quite being able to suppress a slight trembling of his lips, had let him hope, had made him believe . . . and considering besides that this would without doubt have pleased her poor mother . . .

'In short, what is mine from now on will count as yours,' he concluded, lowering his voice.

He leaned a little forward, staring her in the eyes – and it was the first time that he had addressed her with the informal 'tu'! At last, he stood up, and hurriedly excusing himself, promised to be back in the morning.

They had such a lot to talk about!

8.

'We have such a lot to talk about' – Oreste would declare at every leave-taking, or at least his serious tender expression would affirm it.

But the one talking, if the truth be told, was always him.

When he didn't let himself be carried away on the wave of his habitual memories regarding both the years he spent as a boy in the seminary and the war he had later fought in the trenches of the Carso, he embarked on long monologues centred on his religious preferences, and most of all on the recent, decisive political developments, which had such a close bearing on religion.

After the signing of the Lateran Pact, in the February of that year, his patriotism had begun to overflow, liberally, enthusiastically. Good for the Church! – he said – which for the sake of Italy and the world had been able to set aside every trivial doctrinal matter and any sense of rivalry. But good for the Italian State as well, which deserved the highest praise for being the first to set out on the path of reconciliation. And it was clear, while he expressed himself in this manner, that the Church and the State stood before him in the form of a man and a woman, who, leaving behind a prolonged and difficult relationship, often perturbed by violent crises, had finally decided to get married.

And from that point on, how many splendid things would come to pass! – he would pursue the topic with an exultant expression. The spring that was already coming would see the onset of an era of peace and perpetual joy, a return of the legendary golden age. According to the Bible and the evangelist, according to the dream and prophesy of Dante, Church and State would acknowledge each other in perfect accord. The priest would no longer be persecuted nor held in suspicion. Civil society would no longer rebuff him, but welcome him like a father who should be heeded and revered. And if, today, as things stood, the rebirth of an actual and proper Catholic party, one such as the *Partito Popolare*, would be a perilous thing to hope for, it didn't matter: for now the results already achieved were more than enough. It was no little thing, if the truth be told, that the

Catholic Action Party and those young fellows of the *Federazione Università Cattolica Italiana* were to be left in peace! It wasn't a small thing at all, but rather a momentous one, to find oneself able serenely to bless the Fatherland's flag displaying so much of the Savoyan coat-of-arms!

Carried along by the intense emotion these speeches awoke in him, but changing the tone, he would at last begin to talk of the two of them, of him and Lida, and in particular of the small villa outside Porta San Benedetto where in May, the day after their wedding, they would take up residence.

He would complain. He would take issue with the plasterer because a wall freshly skimmed, and seeping moisture, was showing stains in various places; with the carpenter because a shutter didn't close properly; with the surveyor because of his brusqueness and bad manners. But then, as soon as he began to describe the place where the villa was being constructed, how his face would relax and become clear again! The little dwelling was situated at the end of Corso San Benedetto – he repeated for the umpteenth time, and it seemed as though he was girding himself to describe certain very special details, almost arcane ones, of a far-away city, a city infinitely more lovely, agreeable and hospitable than Ferrara. He was referring to that district beyond the walls, situated between the Customs barrier and the railway bridge, where a series of houses large and small had been built in the preceding years. Whether larger or smaller, each had at its disposal its own land, to cultivate as a garden or kitchen garden. The two of them, installed there, would be able to breathe clean air – ah! country air. And here, as though overcome, he would then fall quiet – now that the happiness which they had long been awaiting was already in sight, within his grasp, he evidently preferred not to describe it.

May arrived.

In the last few days Oreste had lost his calm. He seemed suddenly riddled with fear, anxiety. He had always referred indirectly to their marriage: by sign, by indirect allusion, nothing more. Now, however, after having been contented for years by a promise that had not even been made in so many words, after having consented to any prevarication, he wanted to expedite everything, not to lose a single day. The date of the ceremony had been decided some time back: they were to be married the third week of the month. And yet, why not get married earlier? – he found himself suggesting. What else did they have to do in preparation?

Lida stared at him, astonished. She didn't understand.

'Why all this fret just now?' she asked him. 'Why had he changed so much?'

He paused a little before replying. He stared at her with desperation in his eyes, then said slowly: 'I'm like one of those horses that collapse at the finish line.'

He then spoke of marriage, of what marriage meant to him. He said that he considered it the supreme aim of his life, so that only after they were married – not before! – he might perhaps have the courage to ask for Divine Providence to protect them. It was true, he admitted, nodding gravely. Up till now, he had had no rush. But, on the other hand, how could he have pushed things forward, feeling as he did that he couldn't count on his own strength?

Lida heard him out. She still didn't understand. Yet it was enough for her to raise her eyes once more, and she suddenly realized: Oreste was still afraid of losing her! Stretching across the table, she placed her hand on his hands, more tightly clenched than ever in their characteristic convulsion. And a moment later, for the first time, she found herself in his arms.

The years that followed, arduous, calm, largely happy, were marked by no momentous events. Even the winters, Oreste would say – though he was to die quite soon, in the spring of 1938 – even the winters seemed to have finally become more settled.

It's true that every year, towards the end of autumn, he still loved to stand before the window, with the air of a meteorologist. But, of this one could be sure, he did this not because of any doubts about the truth of his predictions, of the now stable, or almost stable good weather, but rather the better to savour the intimate pleasure procured for him by the ownership of a new, modern house equipped with everything necessary for a comfortable life of modest luxury, including an excellent central heating boiler.

Within the Walls

It was evident that the future no longer worried him in any way. After the marriage, Lida had immediately adapted herself to his devout habits, and began regularly to frequent the not-far-off church of San Benedetto, just within the city walls. The thin girl eaten away by anxiety, of those years when he had begun to visit a certain room in Via Salinguerra, had now become a beautiful wife, calm, serene, more than a bit chubby. What else could he desire from then on? What could be better?

Sometimes they joked together about this topic of Lida's beauty.

More inclined to believe it than she tried to appear, she would pull a face.

'Me, beautiful?'

'To say the least!' he would reply, smiling, while, with an expression of pride, he gazed into her eyes.

And yet – he would continue, serious once more – there was absolutely no reason to be surprised by that. This new beauty of hers, so right and timely, so much that of a wife, for which in the end it didn't seem presumptuous on his part to assign himself some portion of the credit, arrived on cue to demonstrate, had there been any such need, that the Good Lord had not only approved their union, but had taken pleasure in it.

9.

'He was happy,' Lida sometimes told herself.

And yet, as soon as she happened to frame these words in her mind, an echo would break in on her to deform and distort them. Flecked with doubt, with painful rancour, the words would change into a question to which no one, herself least of all, would be able to reply other than in the negative.

Poor Oreste. He, too, had not been happy. No. In truth something had always been missing for him as well. Sufficient proof was the tender, more than paternal care that for years, for all the years of their marriage, he had lavished upon Ireneo.

When Ireneo had left the seminary with the intermediate diploma in his pocket, Oreste had immediately taken him on, in the workshop, and had installed him at his own little bench between the trimming machines and the glass door. He had wanted to teach him the trade. And some late afternoons, at dusk, when Lida would cross half of the city to reach the binding shop in Via Salinguerra – later, all three of them would return up the Giovecca or Via Mazzini, but each time passing by in front of the Caffè della Borsa, right in the centre – it seemed to her as though she could still see him as he brooded behind the big bench with his eyes shining with affectionate zeal over that apprentice, who was so sad, so mute, and yet so ready to be distracted by the least thing happening in the square outside. It seemed to her that she could still see him, still hear him: with that vigorous torso of his, out of keeping with his short legs, that loomed up from the stool on the other side of the bench, with his big, hard hands, oddly become more delicate since his marriage vows (he could never be parted from his wedding ring – not even in 1935 at the time of the sanctions!),[1] with his strong, chirpy, piercing voice . . . Oh, how hard he must have struggled so that she, Lida, remained unaware of his desire for a son! How he must have secretly tormented himself, almost as though to punish the desire itself, to smother it within him: at a certain point he had even pressed for Ireneo to assume his surname!

And yet, despite everything, Lida thought, Oreste never gave up hope. For her to be sure of this she only needed to remember the look he gave her every time she entered the workshop: a questioning but calm look, full of unbending faith.

If not now, his look said, then soon, very soon, she would come to him with the great news. She would give him a son, without doubt, a son that was really his, of *his* blood, and thus different physically and in character from the son she had before marrying him, who, although he had given him his own surname, although he was instructing him in his own trade with all the enthusiasm he was capable of, had nevertheless never wanted to call him anything but uncle: 'Uncle Oreste'.

---

[1] In October 1935, in response to Italy's invasion of Ethiopia, the League of Nations began to impose limited sanctions upon Italy.

A son that was really his – Lida pursued the thought – that was what was missing for him, that was the only shadow that had disturbed the serenity of their married life.

Regarding that golden age of which, in February 1929, he had predicted the return, he evidently awaited nothing so eagerly as to hear her declare: 'I'm pregnant.'

It was equally evident, though, that death, taking him by surprise, had prevented the possibility of this hope turning into despair.

The Stroll before Dinner

I.

Even today, rummaging through some small second-hand stores in Ferrara, it's not unlikely that you could turn up postcards almost a hundred years old. They show views that are yellowed, stained, sometimes, to tell the truth, barely decipherable ... One of the many shows Corso Giovecca, the main city thoroughfare, as it was then, in the second half of the nineteenth century. To the right and in shadow, in the wings, looms the buttress of the City Theatre, while the light, typical of a golden springtime dusk of the Emilia Romagna, congregates entirely on the left-hand side of the image. There the houses are low, having for the most part only a single floor, with their roofs covered with thick russet tiles, and below them some little shops, a grocer's store, the entrance to a coal merchant's, a horsemeat butcher and so on: all of which were razed to the ground when, in 1930, the eighth year of the Fascist Era, almost opposite the City Theatre, the decision was made to build the enormous structure of the General Insurance in white Roman travertine.

The postcard has been adapted from a photograph. As such it reveals, and not inaccurately, the look of the Giovecca around the turn of the twentieth century – a kind of wide carriageway amid the rather shapeless surroundings, with its rough cobbles, more fitting for a large village of Lower Romagna than of a provincial capital, divided in the middle by the fine parallel lines of the tram rails – but it also reveals just as clearly how life was going on along the entire street in that moment when the photographer pressed the button. The street thus captured extends from the corner of the City Theatre and the Gran Caffè Zampori beneath it, to the right, a few yards away from where the tripod had been set up, as far down there as the distant, pink sunlit facade of the Prospettiva arch at the very end.

In the foreground the image seems crammed with detail. One can see the boy from the barber shop peeping from the threshold and picking his teeth; a dog sniffing the pavement in front of the entrance to the horsemeat butcher's; a schoolboy running across the street from left to right, just managing to avoid ending up under the wheels of a calèche; a middle-aged gentleman, in frockcoat and bowler hat, who, with lifted arm, pulls back the curtain which shields the interior of the Caffè Zampori from any excessive intrusion of light; a splendid coach and four which is moving forwards at a fast trot to attack the so-called Castle ascent. Except that as soon as one begins to search, perhaps half-closing one's eyes, the slender central space of the postcard which corresponds to the furthest part of the Giovecca, everything then becomes confused, things and people merge together in a kind of luminous dusty haze, all of which would help explain why a girl of around twenty years of age, at that very moment walking quickly along the left-hand pavement, having arrived at not more than a hundred metres from the Prospettiva, would have been unable to transmit as far as us contemporary spectators the least visible sign of her existence.

We should declare right away that the girl was no beauty. Her face was more or less that of many others, neither beautiful nor ugly: rendered, if that's possible, even more average and insignificant by the fact that in those days the use of lipstick, rouge and powder was not generally acceptable among the working classes. Dark-brown eyes in which the beams of youth only rarely shone, and then almost stealthily, with a frightened, melancholic expression, not that different from the sweet, patient look in the gaze of some domestic animals; chestnut-brown hair that, drawn back at the nape, laid bare rather too much of the bulging, bulky, peasant forehead; a squat, busty torso, belted by a black velvet ribbon, that ended in a slender, not to say graceful neck . . . in a fashionable street such as Corso Giovecca, and during, moreover, that especially animated and bustling hour which, in Ferrara, no less today than at that time, has always preceded the intimate evening ritual of supper, it's fair to suppose that even to a less indifferent eye than the photographic lens, the passing by of a girl like this might easily be overlooked.

It now remains to establish what thoughts, on a May evening some seventy years ago, might have been entertained by a girl like this, a trainee nurse of less than three months standing at the City Hospital of Ferrara.

Yet turning back to examine in that same postcard, this time with a slightly warmer sense of real involvement, the general look of Corso Giovecca at that moment of the day and of its history, paying attention to the combined effect of joy, of hopefulness, produced in the very foreground by that blackish spur of the City Theatre, so like a dauntless prow that advances towards freedom and the future, it's hard to dispose of the impression that some tinge of the naive fantasy of a girl – of *that* and no other girl – heading home after many hours of no doubt uncongenial work, will somehow be ingrained within the image we have before us.

At the end of a whole day spent in the sad wards of the ex-convent, where, soon after 1860, the Sant'Anna Hospital had found temporary and inadequate lodging, it was, one could deduce, with real eagerness that Gemma Brondi abandoned herself to her adolescent dreams and imaginings. She would be walking, one might say, without seeing. So much so that, approaching the Prospettiva, when, as was her habit each evening, she mechanically raised her eyes to the three arches of the architectural obstruction, a phrase that was whispered in her ear at that exact moment ('Good evening, Signorina' or something of the kind) found her unready and defenceless, only able to blush and then go pale, and to look around timidly in search of escape.

'Good evening, Signorina,' the voice had whispered. 'Allow me to accompany you.'

The phrase had been this or, as already said, something very similar. Speaking thus, and engaging Gemma Brondi in a conversation that forced her to avoid the black and penetrating eyes of her interlocutor, was a sturdy young man of around thirty years of age, dressed in dark clothes, gripping the handlebars of a heavy Triumph bicycle: a young man with a thin face on which gleamed silver-rimmed spectacles, and a moustache, no less black than his eyes, that drooped around his mouth.

But at this point, travelling at speed along the track which these two young people are about to walk, let us betake ourselves a little way from the Prospettiva on Corso Giovecca, and more particularly inside the big, rustic dwelling where the Brondis, a country family, have lived within the city since time immemorial. The house rises in the shelter of the city walls, separated from them only by virtue of the little dusty street that runs along that stretch of the bastions. It is already almost night. In the ground-floor rooms, whose windows look back towards the open space of the vegetable gardens, they have just now turned on the lights.

2.

The only person in the house who had taken any notice right from the start of Dr Corcos, Dr Elia Corcos, was Ausilia, the elder sister.

Every evening, there she was again.

After having laid the little dining-room's round table, and then, after going into the kitchen and lighting the stove under the pot and the frying pan, as soon as the voices of her father and brothers, who were still working in the vegetable garden in the dark and were now about to come in, began to be more distinctly audible, just at that moment Ausilia vanished, only to reappear later, when the others were about to finish their meal.

Where exactly Ausilia had gone to hide, her mother had almost immediately figured out. But why should she feel any need to speak of it? Seated, in the manner of an *arzdóra*,[2] with the kitchen door at her back, she only allowed herself an inner smile at the image of her eldest daughter leaning on her elbows at the window of the room she shared with her sister, with Gemma, and perhaps unburdening herself of a loud sigh. As regards old Brondi and his three sons, they,

---

[2] Ferrarese dialect word for the formidable peasant housewives of the neighbouring countryside.

bent over their plates, kept on eating with their customary appetite. The novelty of these regular, recurrent disappearances of Ausilia at suppertime seemed not to hold any interest for them. Why should we bother about that? – their aspect seemed to be saying. After a short while, Ausilia, like the capricious spinster she was well on her way to becoming, would reappear of her own accord, whenever it suited her.

Having come down the internal stairs without making the least sound, Ausilia at last presented herself at the doorway of the dining-room, light-footed as a ghost. Her mother was the only one to raise her head. Was this whole affair dragging on? she was silently asking, with the rapid look she threw towards the shadows, where, waiting to approach and be seated, Ausilia usually hovered for a moment. Nor was Ausilia's response ever slow in coming. In acute expectation of the subsequent entry of Gemma, always a bit ruffled and out of breath, Dolores Brondi would receive the information that she sought and that had been weighing on her. No doubt about that, Ausilia would assure her, by her imperceptible grimace of assent. The affair was certainly dragging on, and was showing no signs at all of ending.

Some words passed between mother and daughter about a month later while, as the sun had nearly set, they went to Vespers as usual at the nearby church of Sant'Andrea.

To reach Via Campo Sabbionario where the church was more quickly, they tended to take the path behind the house that led straight across the garden till it reached a small green gate down at the end, situated exactly halfway along the surrounding wall. Who knows? Perhaps it was the narrowness of the path that encouraged them to share these initial confidences, the first exchange of observations and opinions . . . The fact is that, only after the broken, almost fearful sorties of an opening dialogue between the two women, conducted almost at a running pace, without the confidence even to look each other in the face, sorties concerning the looks of Gemma's 'crush' – who, judging by the very pale face and the black moustache that drooped around a carefully shaven chin, could only be a gentleman – only after that was Ausilia allowed to go home, a good twenty minutes before the service's concluding 'Amen'. Her eyes fixed on the altar, Dolores Brondi sensed her getting up, barely displacing the straw seat at her side. True enough – she reckoned, when left alone and gnawed at by a secret envy – it was unlikely the two of them would be able to discuss their new discoveries with the required leisure before the following evening. Soon, anyway, when the thought of Ausilia stationed at her window-observatory had induced her to prolong her conversation with some women of the neighbourhood at the small gate to the vegetable garden a moment or two longer than necessary, if a male voice behind her had shouted from afar, 'And so, are we going to eat?' (till then that had never happened, but it might!), she would have turned back to the house without any hurry, displaying the cold, hostile expression of someone prepared to assert their rights whatever it cost them. Make no mistake about that. She and Ausilia never went out. Never went out, except at the end of the day, and only so as to finish it in a sanctified manner. Who could complain about that? They'd better come armed! If that had happened, supper would have been eaten accompanied by the silence of the tomb. And then, once Gemma had also come back in and she too had finished eating, to bed with everyone.

Summer was approaching. Around the brown, back-lit mass of the apse of Sant'Andrea the bats wheeled, with ever shriller squeaks. And gradually, as time passed, the image of Gemma's suitor was embellished with fresh details: a splendid, swallowtail blue jacket, gleaming silver spectacles, a fat gold watch which he once, at the point of leaving, drew from his waistcoat pocket, and then, as later additions, a white silk cravat, an ivory-handled cane and a manner, what a manner . . . One evening, and this caused Ausilia to draw back in surprise, the couple, rather than down in the street, had appeared above, among the trees on the bastions almost at the height of the window: it might prompt the suspicion that Gemma and the man had been stretched out till then in the thick grass of a meadow to hold and kiss each other – or even worse! Another evening, again on the verge of saying goodbye and leaving, he, besides lifting his cap, had bowed down ceremoniously, perhaps he'd even kissed her hand. His intentions were only too clear! Ausilia, at once awestruck and scandalized, concluded her account of these recent events. Was it possible, though, that Gemma was unaware of the risk she was running? Was it possible she didn't understand that a gentleman like that . . . ? But then who was this gentleman, what was he called?

Of the thirty-year-old Dr Elia Corcos there is no extant portrait. The only one, conserved by Signora Gemma Corcos, during her lifetime, in a small chest of drawers which many years after her death was sold along with other of her belongings to an antiques dealer in Via Mazzini, would be traceable by cutting out a small head from a group photograph, which she, still a girl, a tiny out-of-focus oval among the many, had taken home from the hospital and then hidden in her lingerie drawer. So, just supposing for the sake of pure conjecture that while exploring the insides of a dusty, worm-eaten piece of furniture extracted from the depths of some storeroom it were possible to recover this photograph (a typical keepsake: with ten or so doctors in white coats seated in a semi-circle at the front, and behind, standing, to make a background and as it were a crown, some thirty nurses in grey uniforms), it wouldn't be at all unlikely that, carefully observing the gaunt, hungry and very pale face of Elia Corcos at thirty, one might manage to figure out precisely enough the amazement of Ausilia Brondi to begin with, and very soon after of her mother, when their wide-eyed gaze finally fell on the reality so very different from the one which, little by little, they had built up in their fertile imaginings. 'Huh, just one of those little half-starved doctors from the hospital!' they exclaimed together, galled and disappointed. A nothing, a nobody. Seeing as Gemma hadn't done so, it should be their job to inform the family. Would her father and brothers any longer, from then on, allow Gemma to leave the house? Never mind! So that an affair of this kind be brought to a stop, all of them would gladly have renounced the few coppers she brought home from the Sant'Anna.

Between saying and doing, between the intention and the action, however, there remained the usual shortfall. The truth was that as soon as she returned home (each time, walking along the vegetable garden's narrow path, between the small green gate and the flower bed, had a calming effect on her), Ausilia hurried as usual up to her bedroom and, having replaced the photograph in Gemma's drawer, took up her customary stance at the window.

The thrill of spying and reporting, of conjectures and deductions, the secret delights of fantasy, undermining the severe, intransigent resolution just now formulated, had always deferred it to an undefined future, but as it happened just at the end of that same day all these intentions and prevarications were brought to a sudden halt before the weight of facts.

The enamoured couple were proceeding along the little road without showing any awareness of having arrived at the place where, after glancing up at the blinds from behind which Ausilia was observing them, they would promptly go their separate ways. Gemma was at a slight remove from the doctor, who, though walking at the same pace as her, was separated from her by the bicycle. They were not speaking. But there was something in the stiffness of their carriage, the stubborn way they both kept their gaze fixed on the ground, which conferred a weight and a particular solemnity on their silence. In addition, now they had advanced a bit further, it seemed to Ausilia that her sister's cheeks were streaked with tears.

By this stage they were beneath the window, in front of the doorway. Ausilia suddenly felt herself short of breath. 'What now?' she whispered, pressing a hand to her breast. What did their sudden gaze into each other's eyes mean? And why did they remain separated by the bicycle without saying a word?

Then, as if in response, the doctor picked up the Triumph by the saddle and handlebars, turned it round and quickly leant it against the grassy slope of the bastion on the other side of the road. He stood for a moment there before it, with his back turned and bent over, giving the impression that he was in rapt examination of its chain, or perhaps a pedal. At last, straightening up, he slowly retraced his steps.

Gemma had not moved. With her back to the doorframe, she waited.

The other made a strange gesture: just as though – Ausilia thought – he was combing his moustache.

They kissed for a long time. Again and again.

After which, the doctor once more crossed the road and, having collected the bicycle, wheeled it behind him – time had passed: even in the darkness at the start of the scene it was hard to discern his movements – then he followed Gemma, who had already entered, inside the house.

3.

Brought into the small dining-room and given a seat just in front of the head of the family, who, at his entrance, had raised his eyes from a game of patience and had kept gazing at him with half-open mouth, the doctor began by introducing himself. His name, surname, his parents, his profession, even his address . . . it was a catalogue of personal data of the most official kind: a long stream which, perhaps, had it not been accompanied by the extraordinary, somehow paralyzing courtesy of his manner, or even without the tension which had suddenly gripped the room, might have appeared irksome, pedantic and in its specificity at the very least gratuitous and extravagant.

Elia Corcos – the four males of the house, who until that moment had no clue even about his existence, were in the meantime thinking – what the hell kind of a name is *that*? His doctor's frockcoat; the white silk tie; the black cap with large raised rim which, placed on his tightly pressed knees, stood just proud of the table edge (and everything a bit worn, a touch faded, as though it had been bought secondhand); his eloquence peppered every now and then with brief phrases or single words in dialect, which he pronounced almost shyly, as though he were picking them up with tweezers; his face itself, which seemed fashioned out of a special substance, finer and more fragile than the usual material: however modest his family origins may have been, even if now he was living alone as a bachelor, or whatever his present financial circumstances, everything about him, they were only too aware, spoke of his belonging to a different class, the class of gentlemen, and therefore different, fundamentally alien.

Compared to this fact, every other consideration, including that he wasn't a Catholic but Jewish, or rather an 'Israelite' as he himself termed it, occupied for the moment a very subsidiary position. Apart from the usual, everlasting sense of inferiority, of respect above all created by a timidity as regards speech which always afflicted the country folk, irrespective of whether or not they lived within the city walls, in whatever relations they had with the middle classes, his presence to begin with provoked no special response at all. But what response could it have been expected to provoke at that particular time? The sun of renown, or rather that of an unwearying, affectionate admiration, quite close to fetishistic idolization, which for three entire generations of Ferraresi from all social classes would accompany Elia Corcos throughout his long life – so much so as to make of him a kind of institution, a municipal symbol – the dawning of that sun, which coincided with the dawn of a new century, was still too distant to be observed in the vast sky above the city.

And likewise:

'A great doctor!' would be another accolade, but only to be heard some ten years later, and not before.

Or even some decades later, from witnesses to the flourishing old age of Elia Corcos:

'A genius, gentlemen! A man who if Ferrara had not at that time been Ferrara, but Bologna . . .'

According to the latter, those forever unsatisfied characters, lamenting among other things, the modern decline of Ferrara, always praising and bewailing the distant Renaissance splendours of the house of d'Este, the determining cause of the inadequate (because merely provincial) fortune of Corcos' medical career was a specific historical event that occurred towards the end of the last century.

Around 1890, an obscure Bologna deputy, a Socialist, by 'nefariously' blackmailing Crispi, the great Francesco Crispi, had contrived that the most important northern railway terminus was sited not at Ferrara, but at Bologna. All Bologna's prosperity, all its successive and persisting wealth hinged on that fatal decision, yet the more odious because it had been achieved by the swindle of a Socialist, but for that no whit less advantageous and effective for Bologna, which, thanks to this, became in a trice the major city of Emilia Romagna. So then, like so many of his fellow citizens, like so many equally distinguished gentlemen, guilty of nothing but having been born and brought up in Ferrara, Elia Corcos had only been an innocent victim of political shenanigans. He, too, along with innumerable of his fellow citizens worthy of a better fate, just when he was ready to take flight – Power, Glory, Happiness, and so on: oh, the great eternal words, held back in the throat by fierce pride, but still valid in the imagination, to light up prodigious skies behind the four towers of the Castle that rise in the city centre and give the city's first greeting to whoever enters from the countryside, gloriously bright ... he too, just when everything was at its most promising, had had to renounce, withdraw, surrender. Around the same time he had taken a wife. And his marriage, at the age of thirty, to a working-class girl, undoubtedly gifted with many excellent qualities, though who knows if she even completed the fourth form at middle school, had sealed his defeat and self-sacrifice.

This, then, many decades later, would have been the train of thought of many Ferraresi whose temples had begun to grey between the two wars of this century regarding Elia Corcos and the strange, not to say baffling, marriage of his youth. Having ranged so widely, even evoking the name of Francesco Crispi, these thoughts always led to the same conclusion: that Signora Gemma, the deceased wife of Elia Corcos, had not *understood*, that Gemma Corcos, née Brondi, had not, poor thing, really been the right choice. But was it fair, or useful, to hold her to account in such an unfeeling manner? For a good while she lived alone at the end of Via Borso, at the Charterhouse. And yet had she not been the only person in Ferrara who had ever penetrated the barrier of the solemn, ironical hat raisings which Elia Corcos, especially in the spring, before dinner, strolling along the Giovecca, would habitually dispense to right and left: a barrier of courtesy which had quickly and inevitably blocked any reflex of curiosity, any tentative investigation. And leaving aside once and for all Ferrara and its progressive decline after the Unification, that very evening of 1888 – that far-off summer evening – in the course of which Elia Corcos had asked for her hand and been accepted as her fiancé, who, if not her, was seated in that small, dark, rustic dining-room of the Brondi house between him, Corcos, and her father, at an equal distance from both of them? That place which she occupied was the perfect one to catch the very instant in which, leaning suddenly out of the shadow, the face of the guest had entered, drained, into the circle of light.

Everywhere around was shadow. In the centre the tablecloth shone immaculately.

No, no one was better placed than Gemma Corcos, née Brondi, to appreciate the time required for that sacrifice to be made. The time required by Elia to state the actual reason for his presence – Gemma would recall this to the end of her days – was no more than would be needed to accomplish a brief series of movements: to bend his back, lean his head forward, offer to the light his pale face, a lot paler even than it usually was, as though all the blood in his veins and arteries had suddenly been sucked back into his heart.

What that face declared – the words that tumbled from his mouth didn't count, didn't have the least importance – was: 'Why am I here to ask, as just a moment ago I did ask, that old drunkard for the hand of his daughter the nurse? For what possible motive, in God's name, am I ruining my life by my own hand? Just to make up for a pregnancy? And, to boot, not even one that's "confirmed"?'

And then: 'I still have a choice, should I want it. Changing my mind, I could still leave this place, defy the whole lot of them – father, mother, brother – and never be seen again. As I could, also, should I choose to, play along, from henceforth accept the modest life of a provincial general practitioner, and yet, with the advantage in this case, that when the girl soon accompanies me to the door on to the street, I could start insinuating that she was responsible for *everything*, that it was *they* who in a certain sense forced me into this marriage.'

And then again: 'At this crossroads, the one road rough, hard and uncertain, the other smooth, easy, nice and comfortable, one can't, in all justice, really haver about which to take!'

And finally, while beneath his moustache his lips made a series of lateral tics, clearly sardonic: 'Would you really call it smooth, that road I'm heading down? Nice and comfortable, seriously? Just try it yourself!'

4.

They were married. At first they lodged with his father, Salomone Corcos, the old grain merchant, and there, in Via Vittoria, in the heart of what until not that long before had been the Ghetto, Jacopo was very soon to be born, and then Ruben. Half a dozen years or so would have to pass before the home in Via della Ghiara would be acquired: *'magna, sed apta mihi, sed nulli obnoxia, sed parta meo'*[3] as Elia, whose temples had in the meantime become slightly flecked with white, was wont to say, half seriously, half facetiously.

To arrive there from the Brondi house, after you had got beyond the little alley on top of the bastions and hadn't taken any shortcuts, would require a brisk walk of at least a half hour. You'd begin by leaving behind the Borgo San Giorgio, huddled around the big eponymous church with its brown bell tower. You'd continue by hugging the long, blind and monotonous wall of the mental asylum. At length, on the left, at the furthest extreme of the boundless plain, after the blue, wavy line of the Bologna hills begins to become visible, if you turn your head towards the city, your gaze will immediately be drawn to a grey facade, down there, laced about with Virginia creeper, the green blinds closed to protect the occupants from any intrusion of noise: a facade turned towards the south and so exposed to even the most minimal variation of light, with its blanchings and darkenings, its sudden reddenings and alterations, which very much suggested something living, something human.

If one looked at it, the house, from high up there on the city walls, one would have thought it a kind of farmhouse, with its fine

---

3 *'parva, sed apta mihi, sed nulli obnoxia, sed non sordida, parta meo, sed tamen aere domus'*: 'Small, but adapted to my needs, subject to none, by no means miserable and bought with my own money' is the motto above the door of the house of the poet Ludovico Ariosto in Ferrara. Corcos has curtailed the quotation and has ironically substituted 'magna' (large) for 'parva' (small).

Within the Walls

flowerbed separated from the adjacent vegetable garden by a hedge, and with the vegetable garden that, full of fruit trees and divided by a thin central path, descended way down there to the sturdy surrounding wall. And there was certainly no danger of being intimidated while approaching from this side! thought Gemma's father and brothers, who, on those afternoons when they came to chop wood, never failed to take the path along the wall. While, from up there, communicating by shouts and crude, brazen whistles, they never failed to feel, however confusedly, and without having ever said as much, as though between the look which the building itself from the second-floor windows and the dormer windows above gently levelled at the fields, and that look which a still youthful woman with her bust framed in the first floor's wide-open window directed at them in the distance, through the already darkening air, a relationship of some kind existed, a secret similarity and affinity. She lifted an arm to greet them, and waved with festive insistence. They were welcome! she seemed to be saying. They should come in! Good Lord, didn't they realize that the little gate at the foot of the wall, which allowed entry to the house also from the back, had been left ajar till darkness fell, just so that they could, if they wanted to, pass freely through?

From the opposite side of the house, the front, one would have no idea of all this.

It seemed like a dignified little construction of bare redbrick. And each time it seemed incredible to Elia's relatives, when they came to visit, that the countryside whose existence Via della Ghiara, with its reserved and tranquil but still markedly urban aspect, almost made one forget, actually began no more than some fifty or so metres away, only just beyond the final veil of those mainly middle-class, though in some cases even aristocratic, facades, among which, without being harmed by the comparison, was to be found also that of Dr Corcos.

Corcos, Josz, Cohen, Lattes or Tabet, whichever family it was, none of them, kith or kin, seemed at all intimidated by the brass rectangular plaque on which was inscribed: DR ELIA CORCOS DOCTOR & SURGEON. When properly polished, it stood out on the street door with its fine, black, capital letters. And even if in their time they had severely criticized Elia for having taken a goy as a wife, and following that had also disapproved of his leaving the Ghetto quarter where he was born to establish himself in such a remote area of the city, this nevertheless, it should be added, was always with a secret sense of satisfaction that the main entrance should be so consecrated to him, Elia, and by extension to themselves. The look of the house, the quiet secluded nature of the district, likewise, even in its contrast to the medieval alleyways from which they'd come, was enough to reassure them. It showed that Elia, after all, had not changed, had remained one of their blood and upbringing: finally, unquestionably a Corcos.

This last fact having been firmly established, and since at this point it was clear that when he'd converted he'd hardly even considered it, what's more, with his growing success as a doctor in both the city and the province, he conferred distinction on his shared origins, and his kin sooner or later would enjoy the benefits – at little more than forty years old, apart from being head of the Sant'Anna Hospital, he had become personal physician to the Duchess Costabili, by far the most chic and influential woman of Ferrara, leaving aside that after the premature death of her consort he was perhaps something more than just a personal physician to the duchess . . . So for everything else he could be excused, justified and, in certain particular cases, even applauded.

What the devil did it matter, for example, they would reason, that personally he issued from a less-than-mediocre family, son as he was of that inept fellow Salomone Corcos, that forgettable and undistinguished little merchant who had never done a thing in his life apart from begetting children into the world (he had a good dozen of them!) and ending up as a useless weight on the shoulders of Elia, the last of the series? And the wife he had chosen as well, a goy and, to make it worse, of low extraction (devoted, though, a capable housekeeper, a harder worker you couldn't easily find, or even ever find, and also an incomparable cook), why should she be considered, as many continued to consider her, a kind of lead weight around his feet? No, no. If he, prudent and circumspect as he'd always been, had decided at a certain point to indulge himself in the luxury of a *mésalliance*, rather than having been merely constrained to make amends for a mistake made during one solitary night shift spent in the company of an exuberant girl (to end up in front of the magistrate on this account had never been considered absolutely remiss in Ferrara!), mightn't it be that he had known exactly what he was doing? However it had actually come about, what was important was that he, despite all his eccentricities and oddities – including that of refusing after a certain date to make any contributions towards a bank established by the Italian School Synagogue, affirming that his conscience did not permit him to pretend to a faith in which he didn't believe (except that, regarding circumcision, he was prepared to lend his full support to that small operation and even once to declare openly in the Temple that he wasn't against the 'custom', corresponding evidently to hygienic norms also known in ancient times, and therefore, not unwisely, included within the religion) – what was important in the end was that he, to all intents and purposes, when it came down to brass tacks, continued to conform to the general rules.

And in this respect, in 1902, when little Ruben, only eight years old, died of meningitis, had it not perhaps been for everyone a delightful and consoling confirmation that on that occasion it was actually he, Elia, in contrast to his usual indifference to all things religious, who insisted that his second-born should be interred beside his grandfather Salomone with the most orthodox rites? The goyish wife, no: every now and then she had tried to rebel. Not only had she followed step by step the funeral from Via della Ghiara to the cemetery, but afterwards, when the gravediggers had finished filling in the grave, she had thrown herself with open arms on the mound of fresh earth, to the dismay especially of Dr Carpi, interrupted in the midst of his prayers, and had started crying that she didn't want to leave her baby, her *pòvar putìn*,[4] there. Well, of course a mother's always a mother. But what was she, Gemma, thinking? That a Corcos, rather than in the Jewish cemetery at the end of Via

---

4 Ferrarese dialect: 'Poor little boy'.

Montebello, so intimate, tidy, green and well-tended as it was, should be buried outside the walls, in the endless graveyard of the Charterhouse, where you could spend a whole day just trying to find a gravestone again? And, going back to that fit of weeping, Gemma was surely entitled to that. But her relatives, who arrived in large numbers for the occasion, they and the great horde of friends and acquaintances they dragged along with them, all unaware of the requirement to cover their heads – what made them display such desperation? And that other woman? Who on earth was that odd little woman with a black shawl around her head and that spinsterish air who, helped by Elia and by Jacopo (already so like his father, the boy: dark-haired, pale-faced, refined . . .), was trying in every way possible to lift Gemma up, but she, Gemma, shook her head and refused to get to her feet?

'Ausilia Brondi? Ah yes, her sister.'

Bumping into Ausilia by chance arriving at the door of Via della Ghiara, there was always one of Elia's relatives ready to repeat this phrase. Cowed, Ausilia gathered her shawl around her throat. And at the click which the lock made, opened from the upper floors by a hand-pulled lever, she would hurriedly give way.

She stepped aside, the aged girl, lowering her eyes. How she would have preferred at that moment to return to her own house, her own family! But no: she too ended up going in, gently closing the big door, queuing up on the staircase in a huddled group with the others, who were busy chatting away to each other: she moved according to an instinct that, for at least forty years, had always been stronger than any will she had to resist it, to fight against it.

5.

They would all find themselves together again on the first-floor landing, in front of another closed door. Even here, before someone came to open it, there was always something of a wait.

Finally, they would all be inside. And yet, remaining again behind – the visiting Jewish relatives had immediately gone directly ahead towards the kitchen – it often happened that Ausilia lingered on her own to roam round the rooms of the whole house, including at times those of the second and top floor, avoiding in her wanderings, apart from the storeroom for wood and the pantry on the ground floor, only the grey, half-empty and slightly scary granary under the roof. She would go through room after room, surveying one by one, with a strange kind of envious love, the innumerable familiar objects which cluttered them, the shelves overflowing with books and the notepads scattered everywhere, even in the passageways and in cabinets and cupboards, the ill-assorted furniture, the tables large and small, with the odd, complicated study lamps, the old canvases, nearly all in a parlous state, hung on the walls beside framed and glazed family and hospital photographs, and so on. In the meantime she kept repeating to herself, not without bitterness, that between them, the Brondis, and that tribe, so proud and reserved, who usually treated her as they did, it wasn't possible to reach a real agreement or understanding of any kind that wasn't merely superficial.

Even before seeing him again, she imagined the face of her brother-in-law.

In the big kitchen, where the copper pots and pans reflected back flames from the walls, and where, from his annual summer trips to Baden-Baden or to Vichy in the retinue of the Duchess Costabili, Elia would return every autumn with such an intense and imperious desire for peace and reflection – there, in a few minutes, he would appear to her again, seated as always at the desk placed under the window furthest from the entrance, perhaps just as he lifted his gaze from his books to look out beyond the vegetable garden, beyond the garden wall, which divided it from the bastions, beyond the bastions themselves and to focus finally, smiling vaguely beneath his moustache, on the great golden clouds which filled the skies towards Bologna. Even just to imagine him, Elia, was enough for her to know once and for all that in the big kitchen filled with maids, with nurses from the Sant'Anna Hospital or from his clinic, with various Jewish relatives, with babies and children always shouting, often playing wildly and unrestrainedly, when not even Gemma, although his wife and the woman of the house, had ever managed to penetrate the invisible wall behind which Elia withdrew from everything that surrounded him, she the unmarried sister-in-law would never be able to occupy anything but a place apart, a little, very subsidiary and subordinate space. Her mother had been right to have always refused to enter that house! And her father and brothers, who, when they came there to chop wood, never wanted to go upstairs, so much so that at a certain point food and drink had to be taken down to them in the wood store – weren't they, too, right to avoid any intimacy and confidence?

And yet there had been one who was utterly different from the rest of Elia's relatives – a conviction that the years only strengthened in Ausilia's mind.

The person in question was Elia's father, poor Signor Salomone.

Having been married three times, he had twelve children, and though already very old indeed, and a widower for the third time when Elia got married, and very attached to the rented apartment in Via Vittoria where he had lived for more than half a century, regardless of all this, he had finally agreed to follow his beloved son, the doctor, to the house in Via della Ghiara, just in time, as it happened, to die at almost a hundred years of age.

To give an idea of this personage, let's suppose him out walking. Should he perchance meet a woman whom he knew, it made no difference whether she was wearing the hat of a lady or a proletarian shawl, he would immediately, in a sign of respect, salted with a refined admiration if it was worth the effort, draw back completely against the wall or step down from the pavement. However religious and devoutly practising he was (oh yes, marrying as he did, Elia must have dealt him, at least at first, a heavy blow), he would never speak of religion at home, neither in his own nor in other people's homes. He would speak only in his own particular dialect, similar to Ferrarese, but full of the Hebrew words which were common in the vicinity of Via Mazzini, but that was all. And the fact was that in his mouth even those Hebrew words had nothing strange or mysterious about them. Who knows how, but even they took on the coloration of his continual optimism, his bountiful character.

When asked the time, he would draw from his waistcoat pocket

Within the Walls

a little silver wind-up watch, which at his death would be passed on to Jacopo, his first-born grandson, and, before checking the hour, raise it to his ear with a beatific expression. And often, even if no one had asked him (he was undoubtedly the meekest man, though at the same time a great patriot) he would tell of the distant time when Ferrara was still part of Austria and, in the main square, the white-uniformed soldiers were guarding the Archbishop's Palace with fixed bayonets at the ready. People looked at these soldiers with scorn, with hatred. He too – he admitted – being at that time, before 1860, still quite young, did the same. And yet, thinking back – he would add – they were hardly to blame, those poor lads, mainly Czechs and Croats put there like stakes to prop up the vineyard of the cardinal-legate. Soldiers must do as they're told, after all. Orders are orders.

Even more frequently, however, he would recall Giuseppe Garibaldi, who, he had no difficulty in admitting, had been the sun, the idol of his youth: he dwelt most of all on the general's voice, strong and melodious like the finest of tenors, and such as to rouse the blood, which, one starry night in June of 1863, he, Salomone Corcos, lost in a crowd of enthusiasts, had heard, lift from the balcony of the Palazzo Costabili, where the hero of two worlds had been a guest for the whole week.

He had gone there with Elia when he was a small child, he used to recount, holding him in his arms for the entire duration of his speech, so that the youngest of his children – too young to remember another miraculous night only a few years earlier, when the gates of the Ghetto had been beaten down by the fury of the people – should from that time on preserve indelibly in his memory the image of the red-shirted, blond-haired Man who had created Italy. Garibaldi! He, Salomone, was carrying a not inconsiderable weight of family responsibilities, something like twelve children. And yet he felt that one word from the general – he always spoke haltingly in saying such things but reaching this point in the story he was almost short of breath – would have been enough, had it been necessary, for him to have followed him to the ends of the earth. The ends of the earth, and that's for sure! – he would repeat with shining eyes.

Whoever had heard Giuseppe Garibaldi speaking to the people would have done the same.

With Gemma he had always been gentle, kind and most attentive. And likewise in his relations with her, Ausilia, how affable he had been on every occasion, how courteous! For example: it often happened that, meeting her about the house, he would ask her about the price of vegetables, how much were the peas and the lettuce selling for, how much the potatoes, the beans and so on. But he did this, it was clear, above all to indicate to her that he had the greatest respect and consideration for her family, her family of vegetable farmers. 'You are Ausilia, Gemma's sister,' he might well have begun by saying. And he seemed quite pleased enough to have been able to figure it out on his own – since for some while his head, he explained, tapping his forehead with a finger and smiling, had been a bit faulty now and then.

But there was something of him, apart from his white curls shiny as silk, and his characteristically big nose, which she recalled in a special way. And that was the smell that wafted from his clothes.

A vague mixture of citrus fruits, of old grain and hay, it had the same smell which she had always noticed when she flicked through the ancient, indecipherable pages of some little books of Jewish rites that he brought with him to the house in Via della Ghiara, for their 'eventual' distribution among the guests for the two suppers that followed Passover. They were illustrated by blueish, slightly faded engravings which showed, according to what one could read in the Italian printed beneath each of them, the Ten Plagues of Egypt, Moses before Pharaoh, the Passage through the Red Sea, the Rain of Manna, Moses on the Peak of Sinai speaking with the Eternal, the Adoration of the Golden Calf: and so on up until the Revelation to Joshua of the Promised Land. Elia's frockcoat never smelled of anything but ether and carbolic acid. The clothes and the entire person of Salomone Corcos, by contrast, exhaled a perfume that, for all its different accents, reminded her of incense.

Placed in a chest of drawers in the so-called 'good' room, a big shadowy place overlooking Via della Ghiara where no one ever set foot, the ritual Passover books had impregnated not just the

Within the Walls

furniture but the whole atmosphere with this perfume. Whenever she, Ausilia, went to shut herself up in there, remaining, seated in the darkness, to think over her own concerns for hours on end sometimes (she had continued to use this room as a kind of hiding-place even after the death of Gemma when, in 1926, she had come to live with Elia and Jacopo as housekeeper, and even after both of them were deported to Germany in the autumn of 1943 . . .), she would always have the feeling that poor Signor Salomone was there too, within the four walls, present in flesh and blood. Just exactly as if, still in this world and silently breathing, he was seated beside her.

6.

Love was something different, Ausilia reflected – no one knew that better than her.

It was something cruel, atrocious, to be spied on from a distance, or to be dreamt of beneath lowered eyelids.

In fact, the secret feeling that from the very start had kept her bound to Elia, strong enough to force her for her whole life to be continuously, fatally, indispensably present, had certainly never given rise to the least joy. No, truly it hadn't, if every time she entered the big kitchen of the house in Via della Ghiara where, near the window in the corner, he would linger over his studies until suppertime (he would study and seemed to notice nothing, and yet nothing really worth the trouble of being noticed would ever escape his intensely black, piercing, investigating eyes . . .), she felt a need to avoid that calm gaze which for a moment, at her entrance, had detached itself from a book, and the need quickly to summon, as if to defend her, the good and kind image of Salomone Corcos.

The gaze of Elia! Nothing could really escape it. And yet at the same time he seemed hardly to see anything . . .

That famous night on which he became engaged to Gemma (it happened in 1888, in August), and having returned very late, he passed his father's bedroom on tiptoe, he stopped there for a moment, wondering whether to go in. Extract the tooth and be rid of the pain, he thought to himself. Perhaps it was best to tell his father everything straight away.

He was about to lower the door handle when from the other side he was taken aback by his father's voice.

'Good Lord, where on earth have you been?' he cried out. 'D'you know that I haven't been able to get a wink of sleep?'

These words of his father, and especially the keening tone of his voice, made him change his mind. Having climbed up to his own room, a little room which looked out over the roofs, the first thing he did was to open the window and lean out. Realizing it was already dawn (not a murmur from within the house, the city asleep at his feet, and down there one of the four towers of the Castle touched at its very tip by a fleck of pink light), he suddenly decided not only to forgo any sleep but without further delay to start studying.

Science – he then said to himself. Wasn't Science his real calling?

It would be he, several decades later as Ausilia recalled, who told her all this, unprompted, at the end of one of the usual suppers that the two of them would take in the kitchen.

He was in front of her, the other side of the table, his face fully lit by the lamp above. While he spoke, grinning slightly beneath his big, brilliantly white moustache, he seemed to be watching her.

But did he actually see her? *Truly* see her?

It was – poor Gemma – certainly a very odd expression that he had in his eyes at that moment! It was as if, from the morning following the evening on which he'd promised her sister to marry her, as if from then on he had looked at things and at people in just that way: from above and, in some way, from beyond time.

A Memorial Tablet in Via Mazzini

I.

When, in August 1945, Geo Josz reappeared in Ferrara, the only survivor of the 183 members of the Jewish community whom the Germans had deported to Germany in the autumn of 1943, and all of whom were generally believed to have ended up in the gas chambers, no one in the city at first recognized him.

Josz. The surname certainly sounded familiar, having belonged to that Angelo Josz, the renowned salesman of wholesale fabrics, who, although a Fascist at the time of the March on Rome, and even remaining in the Ferrarese circle of friends around Italo Balbo at least until 1939, hadn't, for all of that, managed to protect himself and his family from the great raid and round-up that occurred four years later. Yet how could one believe – many immediately objected – that this man of uncertain age, enormously, absurdly fat, who'd appeared a few days earlier in Via Mazzini right in front of the Jewish Temple had turned up alive from no less a place than the Germany of Buchenwald, Auschwitz, Mauthausen, Dachau, and so on, and above all that he, he of all people, was seriously one of the sons of poor Signor Angelo? And then, even conceding that it wasn't all a sham, a fabrication, that among that group of Jewish townsfolk sent off to the Nazi death camps there might indeed have been a *Geo* Josz, after so much time, so much suffering dealt out more or less to everyone, without distinction of political affiliation, wealth, religion or race, what did this character want just then, at that particular time? What was he after?

But better to proceed in an ordered manner, and, tracking a little way back into the past, to begin with the first moment of Geo Josz's reappearance in our city: the moment where the story of his return should properly begin.

To write an account of it, there's the risk that the scene might look rather implausible, a piece of fiction. Even I have doubts about its veracity every time I consider it within the frame of what for us is that familiar, usual street: Via Mazzini, the street, that is, which leaving the Piazza delle Erbe, and flanking the quarter of the erstwhile Ghetto – with the San Crispino Oratory at the start, the narrow cracks of Via Vignatagliata and of Via Vittoria halfway down, the baked-red facade of the Jewish Temple a little further on, as well as, along its entire length, the crowded rows of stores, shops and little outlets facing each other – still serves today as the main route between the historic centre and the Renaissance and modern parts of the city.

Immersed in the brilliance and silence of the early afternoon, a silence which at wide intervals was interrupted by gunshots, Via Mazzini seemed empty, abandoned, preserved intact. And so too it appeared to the young worker who, from one-thirty on, mounted on some scaffolding with a newspaper hat covering his head, had been busy about the marble slab which he'd been employed to affix at two metres height on to the dusty brickwork of the synagogue's facade. His appearance was that of a peasant forced by the war to seek work in the city and stand in as a plasterer, but whatever the tell-tale signs of this were, they would be obliterated in the blazing light, as he himself was well aware. Nor was this annihilating effect of the big August sun at all counteracted by the small group of passers-by, various in colour and behaviour, which had gathered on the cobblestones behind his back.

The first to stop were two young men, two partisans with beards and spectacles, in short trousers, red scarves round their necks, submachine guns on gun-belts: students, city gents – the young peasant plasterer had thought, hearing them talk and turning for a moment to peek at them. Soon afterwards they were joined by a priest in his black vestments, undaunted by the outrageous heat, and then a sixty-year-old from the middle classes with a pepper-and-salt beard, a jovial air, his shirt open to reveal the skinniest chest and a restless Adam's apple. The latter, after having begun to read in a low tone what was presumably written on the tablet, name after name, had interrupted himself at a certain point by exclaiming with emphasis: 'A hundred and eighty-three out of four hundred!' as if those names and those numbers might have a direct bearing also on him, Podetti Aristide from Bosco Mésola, who found himself in Ferrara by chance, and had no intention of staying a day longer than was necessary, and meanwhile was minding his own business and nothing else. Jews, he now heard it said by a growing number of people. A hundred and eighty-three Jews deported to Germany, who died there, in the usual way, out of the four hundred who lived in Ferrara before the war. So that was cleared up. But just a second. Since those hundred and eighty-three must have been sent to Germany by the Fascists of the Republic of Salò, what if one day or another they, the *tupín*,[5] should return to take control, and were biding their time in the hope of a return match? It was a fair bet that they'd been walking around the streets for some time and in all likelihood they'd have one of those red handkerchiefs round their neck! Taking that into account, wasn't it better that the Jews, too, pretended not to know anything about it? Ah the *tupín*! You can imagine that at the right moment they could suddenly resurface, clad once more in their mud-camouflage uniforms, with those death's heads on their fezzes and pennants! No, no. Given the state of things, the less one knew about who was a Jew and who wasn't, the better, for all concerned.

And it was that unfortunate boy, so determined to know nothing, as he was happy enough to be working and wasn't interested in anything else, and so diffident about whatever else was going on, imprisoned in his rough Delta dialect as he turned his back to the sun, who, at a certain point, feeling his calf touched – 'Geo Josz?' asked a mocking voice – twisted round, suddenly, annoyed.

Before him stood a short, thickset man, his head covered up to his ears by an odd fur beret. How fat he was! He seemed swollen with

5 Ferrarese dialect for 'mice', but here referring to the Fascist-appointed squads of armed teenagers who patrolled the streets of Ferrara in the latter stages of the war.

water, a kind of drowned man. Still, there was no reason to be scared as, surely to win his sympathy, the man was laughing.

His look turned serious and he pointed at the tablet.

'Geo Josz?' he repeated.

He began to laugh again. But quickly, as if contrite, and seeding his speech with frequent 'Pardon me's' in the German fashion – he expressed himself with the elegance of a drawing-room orator of another age, and Podetti Aristide stood listening to him with his mouth agape – he confessed himself unhappy, 'Believe me', to have disrupted everything with an intervention which had, he was more than ready to recognize, all the qualities of a gaffe. Ah well – he sighed – the tablet would need to be remade, given that the Geo Josz, up there, to which in part the tablet was dedicated, was no other than himself, in flesh and blood. Unless that is he immediately added while surveying them all with his blue eyes – unless the civic committee, accepting the fact as a hint from destiny, didn't immediately give up the whole idea of a commemorative tablet, which – he grinned – even though being affixed in that busy place of concourse it would offer an indubitable advantage, almost forcing passers-by to read it, would have had the adverse effect of clumsily altering the plain, honest facade of 'our dear old Temple', one of the few things remaining the same as 'before' in Ferrara, thanks be to God, one of the few things that one could still rely on.

'It's a bit like you,' he concluded, 'with that face, with those hands, being forced to wear a dinner jacket.'

And so saying he showed his own hands, calloused beyond imagining, but with their backs so white that a identification number tattooed on to the skin, soft, as if boiled, a little above the right wrist, could be distinctly read: with its five numbers preceded by the letter 'J'.

2.

Thus, then, as if, pallid and swollen, he had emerged from the depths of the sea – his eyes a watery cerulean coldly looked up from the

Within the Walls

foot of the low scaffolding: not at all threatening, but rather ironic, even amused – Geo Josz reappeared in Ferrara, among us.

He came from far away, from much further away than he had actually come. Returned when no one expected him; what was it he wanted now?

To face a question of this kind with the requisite calm would have needed a different time, a different city.

It would have needed people a little less scared than those from whom the city's middle class devolved their opinions (among them were the usual lawyers, doctors, engineers and so on, the usual merchants, the usual landowners; not more than thirty, to count them one by one . . .): all good folk who, although they had been convinced Fascists until July 1943, and then from December of that same year, had in some fashion said yes to the Social Republic of Salò, for more than three months had seen nothing but traps and pitfalls all around them.

It's true, they would admit, they had taken the membership card for the Republic of Salò. Out of a civic sense they'd taken it, out of patriotic sentiments, and in each and every case not before the fatal 15 December, in Ferrara, and the following outbreak across all of Italy of the fratricidal struggle.

But to get quickly to the point about that young fellow Josz, they would continue, raising their heads and swelling their chests under jackets in the buttonholes of which some of them had attached whatever decoration happened to be at hand – what was the sense in his going on covering his head, regardless of the stifling August heat, with a big fur cap? And his endless grinning? Instead of behaving in that manner, he would have done far better to explain how on earth he'd become so fat. As till then no one had heard of an oedema brought on *by hunger* – this must have been a joke put about in all likelihood by himself, the one most concerned – his fatness could only mean one of two things: either that in German concentration camps one didn't suffer from the terrible hunger that was claimed in the propaganda, or that he had managed, who knows at what price, to enjoy a very special and respectful treatment. So surely he should behave himself, and stop going around annoying people? Those who go seeking the mote in other people's eyes should look to the proverbial beam in their own.

And what could be said of the others – a minority, to tell the truth – who barricaded themselves in their houses with their ears peeled to catch the least sound from outside?

Among them, there was one with the tricolour scarf around his neck who had offered to preside at the public auctions for the goods sequestrated from the Jewish community, including the furnishings, the silver candelabras and everything from the two synagogues, one above the other, in the Temple of Via Mazzini; and there were those who, covering their white hairs with Black Brigade caps, had undertaken the role of judges in a special court responsible for various executions by firing squad, who had shown, it seemed, no prior sign at all of being in any particular way interested in politics, but rather, in the majority of cases, had led a largely retired life, dedicated to their families, their professions, their studies ... And yet they were so frightened for themselves at this point, so fearful they might unexpectedly be called to account for their actions, that when Geo Josz, too, asked no more than to live, to start living again, even in such a simple, such a basic request, they would have found something to feel personally threatened by. The thought that one of them on a dark night might be secretly taken out by the 'Reds', led to the slaughter in some godforsaken place in the country, this terrible thought returned persistently to unsettle and torment them. To stay alive, to keep going in any way possible. They needed to survive. At any cost.

If only that wreck, they would snort, would take himself off, would get the hell out of Ferrara!

Unbothered that the partisans, appropriating what was the HQ of the Black Brigade, were using the house in Via Campofranco still owned by his father, and therefore now his, his alone, as their barracks and prison, he made do with carting around his ominous face everywhere it wasn't wanted: with what transpired to be the quite evident aim of continually goading those who, sooner or later, would have to settle all of his accounts. It was scandalous, any road, that the new authorities should put up with this state of affairs without so much as batting an eyelid. It would be useless appealing to the prefect, Dr Herzen, who the day after the so-called Liberation had been made president by that same *Comitato di Liberazione Nazionale*[6] over which, after the events of 15 December 1943, he had secretly presided – useless because, if it was true, which it certainly was, that every night in secret conclave they updated lists of proscribed persons in his office in the castle . . . Oh yes, how well they knew that kind of person who, in 1939, had let himself be evicted without a word of protest, as though it were nothing, from the shoe factory a couple of kilometres along the road to Bologna, near Chiesuol del Fosso, which at that point he owned, and which later, during the war, had ended up as a pile of rubble! With his half-bald head, his feeble pretence of being a good paterfamilias, with his eternal smile full of gold teeth, with his fat lenses for myopia encircled by tortoiseshell rims, he presented that characteristically meek aspect (apart from the rigid straight spine which seemed screwed to the bicycle saddle he was inseparable from: a spine that was so in keeping with his Jewish surname, with its not-so-distant German origin . . .) of all who should be seriously feared. And what about the archbishopric? And the English governership? Wasn't it precisely the unfortunate sign of the times that even from such quarters there was never any response, apart from a sigh of desolate solidarity or, worse, a smile poised between mockery and embarrassment?

You can't reason with fear and with hatred. Though had they wanted to understand with the minimum of effort what was turning over in the soul of Geo Josz, it would have been enough for them to return to the moment of his first reappearance in front of the Jewish Temple in Via Mazzini.

That moment will perhaps be best recalled by the middle-class man of about sixty years of age, the one with the sparse little greying beard and the dry-skinned throat, who was among the first to stop under the commemorative tablet for the Ferrarese Jews deported to Germany, raising his shrill voice ('A hundred and eighty-three out of

---

6 The Committee for National Liberation was formed in September 1943 in opposition to Italian Fascism and the German occupation.

four hundred!' he had proudly cried out) to call the attention of all present to the importance of its inscription.

Having been present in silence when the sixteen-year-old survivor made a display of his hands, he immediately made his way through the small crowd to kiss him noisily on the cheeks, the latter, however, with his hands and forearms still nakedly extended before him, merely exclaimed in a noticeably cold tone, 'With that ridiculous little beard, my dear Uncle Daniele, I didn't recognize you.' A phrase which should have at once been considered very telling indeed. And not only about his identity.

And so he continued: 'Why the beard? Have you perhaps decided that a beard suits you?'

Tightening his lips, he was surveying with a critical eye all the beards of various thickness and measure which the war, rather like the profusion of fake identity cards, had made such a common feature also in Ferrara – it really seemed as if he were only concerned with that. But rather than the beards it was clear that there was something else, everything else that was troubling him.

In the immediate vicinity of that which, before the war, had been the Josz house, at whose door uncle and nephew presented themselves that same afternoon, there were to be seen, naturally, a good number of beards. And this contributed not a little in giving to the low building of exposed red brickwork, topped by a slender Ghibelline tower and extensive enough to cover almost the entire length of the secluded Via Campofranco, a grim, military air, fitting perhaps to recall the old owners of the establishment, the marqueses Del Sale, from whom Angelo Josz had bought it in 1910 for a few thousand *lire*, but it didn't in the slightest remind one of him, the Jewish wholesale-cloth dealer who ended up in Germany with his wife and children.

The big street entrance door was wide open. In front of it, seated on the steps, with machine-guns between their bare legs or lounging on the seats of a jeep parked by the high wall opposite which encircled a huge, burgeoning garden, a dozen partisans were lazing about. But there were others, in greater numbers, some with voluminous files under their arms and all with energetic, determined faces, who kept coming and going. Between the street, half in shadow, half in

Within the Walls

sunlight, and the wide-open entrance of the old baronial house, in short, there was an intense, vivid, even joyful bustle, fully in keeping with the shrieks of the swallows that swooped down, almost grazing the cobblestones, and with the clacking of typewriters that issued ceaselessly from the barred ground-floor windows.

When this odd couple, one tall, thin and wild-looking, the other, fat, sluggish and sweaty, finally decided to step inside the entrance, they immediately attracted the attention of that company – nearly all of them boys, mostly bearded and long-haired, and armed. They gathered round, some rising from the rough benches placed along the walls. And Daniele Josz, who clearly wanted to show off to his nephew his familiarity with the place and its new occupants, was already briskly replying to every question.

By contrast Geo Josz kept silent. He stared one by one at those suntanned, rosy faces which pressed up close to them, as if through the beards, beneath them, he hoped to discover some hidden secret, to investigate some taint.

'And they haven't even offered me a drink,' his smile seemed to be saying.

Having become aware, at a particular moment, with a sidelong glance whose meaning was clear, that beyond the vestibule, right at the centre of the adjacent, rather dark and narrow garden in disarray, there still shone a big, full magnolia, he seemed to grow more contented and calm. But that only lasted a moment. Since very soon after, upstairs in the office of the young *Associazione Nazionale Partigiani d'Italia*[7] Secretary for the region (who in a couple of years would become the most brilliant Communist deputy in all of Italy, so very kind, courteous and reassuring as to provoke wistful sighs from not a few young women of the city's best families), Geo repeated with a slight sneer: 'You know that beard of yours doesn't suit you at all.'

It was at this moment, however, in the embarrassed chill that suddenly fell upon what, until then, mainly to the credit of Uncle Daniele, had been quite a cordial conversation, in the course of which

---

7 *ANPI* – the National Association of Italian Partisans – was a partisan organization formed in 1944.

the future honourable gentleman had brushed aside the polite 'lei' form used by the survivor, insisting on the 'tu' of contemporaries and party comrades, that the motive for which the other was there suddenly became clear. If only all those who in the following days built up so many futile suspicions about him had been present at this point.

That house, his look seemed to say as it shifted away from the typist on whom it had alighted and became suddenly menacing (so much so that the girl at once stopped tapping on the keys), that house where *they*, the Reds, had settled themselves in for more or less three months, replacing those *others* who had occupied it before – that is, the Blacks, the Fascists – actually belonged to him, had they forgotten? By what right had they taken possession of it? Both she, the graceful secretary, and he, the likeable and hearty partisan chief, so determined to their credit to make a new world, of a sudden became very careful about how they spoke. What were they thinking? That he would be happy to be lodged in a single room in the house? And would that be the very room in which they were speaking? Was that the one they had in mind to keep him quiet and on his best behaviour? If so, they were seriously mistaken.

There was a big sing-song going on down in the street:

> The wind blows and the storm howls,
> Our shoes have holes, but we must march on . . .

Not a chance. The house was his, make no mistake. They would have to give it back, lock, stock and barrel. And as soon as possible.

3.

During the wait for the Via Campofranco establishment to return effectively and entirely into his possession, Geo Josz seemed happy to occupy a single room. To be a guest.

More than a room, in effect it was a kind of granary built at the top of the crenellated tower that overshadowed the house: a big,

Within the Walls

bare room into which, after having climbed not less than a hundred steps that ended in a rickety, little wooden staircase, one entered directly into a space once used as a lumber-room. It had been Geo Josz himself, with the disgusted tone of someone resigned to the worst, who had been the first to speak of that 'makeshift' solution. All right then, he would adapt himself for the moment, he had said with a sigh. But on the understanding, it should be made very clear, that he could also make use of the lumber-room which was beneath the actual granary, where ... At this point, without finishing the sentence, he lapsed into a brief, mysterious grin.

From that height, however, through a wide window, it was soon apparent that Geo Josz could follow everything that happened not only in the garden, but also in Via Campofranco. And since he hardly ever left the house, presumably spending hour after hour looking at the vast panorama of russet tiles, vegetable gardens and the distant countryside which extended beneath his feet, his continual presence became for the occupants of the floors beneath, to put it mildly, annoying and irksome. The cellars of the Josz house, all of which opened on to the garden, had been made over into secret prison cells in the era of the Black Brigade. About these, even after the Liberation, many sinister stories continued to circulate in the city. But now, under the probably treacherous surveillance of the guest in the tower, evidently they could no longer serve the purposes of secret and summary justice for which they had once been destined. With Geo Josz installed in that sort of observatory, and perhaps, as was attested by the light of the oil lamp which he kept lit from the first signs of dusk until dawn, vigilant at night also, now there was no chance of relaxing, not even for a moment. It must have been two or three o'clock in the morning after the evening when Geo Josz had appeared for the first time in Via Campofranco, when Nino Bottecchiari, who had stayed up working in his office until that time, had, as soon as he'd reached the street, raised his eyes to the tower. 'Beware, all of you!' warned the light of the survivor suspended in mid-air against the starry sky. Bitterly reproaching himself for his culpable frivolity and acquiescence, but at the same time, like a good politician, preparing himself to confront a new reality, the young, future honourable gentleman, with a sigh, climbed on board the jeep.

But it also happened that, at the most unsuspected times of day, Geo soon began to appear on the stairs or down at the entrance, walking past the partisans permanently assembled there and wearing the usual minimal uniforms, clad in impeccable olive-coloured gabardines which almost immediately had replaced the bearskin, leather jackets and tight, calf-hugging trousers they had when they arrived in Ferrara. He would slope off without greeting anyone, elegant, scrupulously shaved, with the rim of his brown felt hat on one side tilted down over his ice-cold eye. By the silence and unease provoked each time he appeared, from the outset he displayed his authority as the house-owner, too well brought up to argue but assured of his rights which his mere presence sufficed to assert and to remind the inconsiderate and defaulting tenant that enough was enough, he should clear out. The tenant shilly-shallies, pretends not to notice the steady protest of the proprietor, who for the moment is saying nothing, but the time is sure to arrive when he calls him to account for the ruined floors, the scratched walls and so on, so that month by month his position worsens, becomes ever more uncomfortable and precarious. It was late, the day after the 1948 elections, when much in Ferrara had already changed, or rather changed back to how it was before the war (yet the deputyship of the young Bottecchiari had by then triumphantly arrived in port), when the *ANPI* decided to transfer its premises to the three rooms of the ex-Fascist headquarters on Viale Cavour, where since 1945 the local employment federation had established itself. Due to the silent and implacable behaviour of Geo Josz, this transferral already seemed more than a little unresponsive and tardy.

He hardly ever went out, as if to make sure that no one in the house should forget him even for a moment. Yet this didn't stop him every now and then from being seen in Via Vignatagliata, where since September he had been granted permission that his father's warehouse, in which the Jewish community had been piling the goods that had been stolen from Jewish houses during the Salò period and had remained for the most part ownerless, should be cleared 'due to absolutely indispensable and urgent restoration work', as he wrote in a letter, 'and for the re-opening of the business'. Or more rarely he might be seen along the Corso Giovecca – with the uncertain step of someone advancing into forbidden territory and whose mind is divided between the fear of unpleasant encounters and the bitter desire, perfectly contrary, to have them – taking the evening *passeggiata* which had been resumed in the city centre, as lively and vibrant as ever; or else at the hour of the aperitif, at a table at the Caffè della Borsa in Corso Roma, sitting down abruptly, as he would always arrive out of breath and drenched with sweat. His attitude of ironical scorn which soon enough had even prompted Uncle Daniele, so expansive and electrified by the atmosphere of those early post-war days, to give up on any conversation through the trapdoor above his head hardly seemed to have discouraged the show of cordial salutations, the affectionate greetings of 'Welcome back!' which now, after the initial uncertainty, began to rain in on him from all sides.

They stepped out from the entrances of the shops next to the warehouse, hands outstretched with the air of people ready for any moral or material sacrifice, or crossed the Giovecca, despite its breadth, and with excessive, histrionic gestures threw their arms round his neck; or they leapt out from the Caffè della Borsa, still immersed in that same subversive half-darkness of the depths in which once, every day at one o'clock, had issued the radio announcements of military defeats (announcements that had barely reached the bike of the boy Geo in the days when he'd sped past . . .), to sit by his side under the yellow awning, which was inadequate protection not only against the blinding glare but also against the dust which the wind swept up in broad whirls from the ruins of the nearby quarter of San Romano. He had been at Buchenwald and – the only one – had returned, after having suffered who knows what torments of body and soul, after having witnessed who knows what horrors. So they were there, at his service, all ears to hear him. He recounted; and they – also to show their contrition at having been so slow to recognize him – would never tire of hearing him, willing even to renounce the lunch to which, tolling twice, the Castle clock above was calling them. While they displayed, almost in testimony of their good faith and in support of the evolution that their ideas had undergone in those terrible, formative years, the rough canvas trousers, the desert jackets with rolled-up sleeves, open collars without a trace of tie, feet slipped without socks into shoes and sandals resolutely unpolished, and, of course, beards – there wasn't one of them without a beard – it was as if they were all saying in unison: 'You've changed, don't you see? You've become a man, by God, and fat as well! But see – we too have changed, time has passed for us too . . .' And they were undoubtedly sincere in exhibiting themselves for the examination and judgement of Geo, and sincere in being pained by his inflexible rejection of their overtures. Just as likewise sincere, in its way, was the conviction held, at least in part, by everyone in the city, even those who had most to fear from the present and most to doubt from the future, the conviction that, for good or bad, from now on there was going to begin a new era, incomparably better than that other one which, like a long sleep filled with atrocious nightmares, was ebbing away in their blood.

As regards Uncle Daniele, who for three months had been living on his wits without knowing each morning where he would be sleeping that night, and so the suffocating cubby-hole in the tower had at once seemed to his incurable optimism a marvellous acquisition, no one was more convinced than he that with the end of the war had begun the glad era of democracy and of universal brotherhood.

'Now at last one can breathe freely!' he had ventured the first night that he'd come into possession of his little cell. He spoke these words, supine on a horsehair mattress, with his hands gripped behind his neck.

'Now at last one can breathe freely, aah!' he had repeated more loudly.

And then: 'Doesn't it seem to you, Geo,' he had continued, 'that the atmosphere in the city is different, really different than before? It can't be denied. Only freedom can produce such miracles! As for me, I'm really convinced . . .'

What Daniele Josz was really convinced about, however, must have seemed of quite dubious interest, as the only reply Geo vouchsafed to the impassioned apostrophes of his uncle from the opening to which the little staircase climbed was either a 'Hmm!' or a 'Really?', which hardly inspired further utterance. 'What on earth will he do?' the old man asked himself, growing silent, while his eyes turned towards the ceiling to follow the slapping back and forth of a pair of indefatigable slippers. And for a short while at least he abstained from further comment.

It seemed inconceivable to him that Geo did not share his enthusiasms.

Having fled from Ferrara during the days of the armistice, he had spent more than a year hidden in an obscure village in the Tuscan-Emilian Apennines, looked after by peasants. Up there, after the death of his wife, who, poor thing, had had to be buried under a false name in the little graveyard, he had joined up with a small band of partisans, assuming the role of political commissar – a circumstance which would soon allow him to be among those suntanned and bearded men who, perched on top of a lorry, would be the first to enter liberated Ferrara. What unforgettable days those were! What joy it had been for him once again to be in the city, half in ruins it's true, almost unrecognizable, but utterly cleared of all the Fascists of every kind, the early enrolled as well as the late! What a pleasure to once again be able to sit at a table in the Caffè della Borsa (a place where no sooner had he arrived than he had chosen it as the premises for resuming his old, modest insurance business) without any threatening look to chase him away, but rather finding himself the centre of a general sympathy! But Geo? – he wondered. Was it possible that Geo felt nothing of what he himself had felt some months before? Was it possible that having descended into hell and by some miracle returned, he should feel no impulse beyond that of motionlessly reliving the past, as witnessed by the frightening series of photographs of his dead – Angelo and Luce, his parents, and Pietruccio, his little brother who was just ten years old – which one day when he had stealthily slunk up to the big room he had found decorating all four of its walls? And finally, was it possible that the only beard in the whole city that Geo found bearable was that of the old Fascist Geremia Tabet, his father's brother-in-law, so esteemed by the regime that he managed to keep on frequenting even the Merchants' Club, at least every now and then, for at least two years after 1938? The night after the day of Geo's reappearance, he, Daniele Josz, with profound unease, had had to follow him to the Tabet house, in Vicolo Mozzo Roversella, where before then he had never dreamt of setting foot. And then, wasn't it shocking that Geo, when the old Fascist stuck his nose out of a first-floor window, had let forth a shrill cry, ridiculously, hysterically, almost wildly impassioned? And what was that cry for? What did it mean? Did it mean perhaps that Geo, despite Buchenwald and the extermination of his whole closest family, had become what his father, poor Angelo, had continued being in all ingenuousness till the very end, even perhaps up till the threshold of the gas chamber: a 'patriot', as he frequently loved to declare himself with such stalwart pride?

'Who's there?' had asked the hesitant, worried voice above.

'It's me, Uncle Geremia, it's Geo!'

They were standing below in front of the big closed door of the Tabet house. It was ten o'clock at night and one could hardly see down in the alley. Geo's strangled cry, Daniele Josz recalled, had taken him by surprise, pushing him into a state of extreme confusion. What should he do? What could he say? But there was no time to consider. The big door had opened and Geo, having rapidly entered, was already striding up the dark stairs. He needed to run after him, at least try to reach him.

He managed to do so only at the second staircase, where, to make things worse, before the opened doorway to the apartment, Geremia Tabet himself stood waiting. With the light from inside at his back, the old Fascist, in slippers and pyjamas, was staring at the two of them, perplexed but not dumbfounded, having resumed his habitual calm.

He had stopped at the edge of the landing, half-hidden in the shadow. When he had seen Geo, who, by contrast, had kept advancing and abruptly clasped his uncle in a frenetic embrace, the latter suddenly felt himself again to be the poor relative whom all of them (his brother-in-law Angelo perfectly in agreement about this along with his wife's family) had always kept at a distance mainly because

Within the Walls

of his political convictions. No, no, Daniele said to himself at this point – not even on this occasion was he going to enter *that* home. Turning his back, he would have walked away. But, instead, what did he do? Instead, like the idiot he was, he had done the opposite. At his final reckoning, he had thought, poor Luce, Geo's mother, was a Tabet. Who can tell – perhaps it was the memory of his mother, Geremia's sister, that kept Geo from treating the nasty Fascist of the family with the coldness that type of character deserved? Natural enough in the circumstances, after the first affectionate greetings had been exhausted, it wouldn't be surprising that the boy should collect himself and re-establish the right distance . . .

But in this he was to be sadly disappointed. For the rest of the visit, which lasted late into the night (as it seemed that Geo couldn't bring himself to leave), he had had to witness, seated in a corner of the small dining-room, shows of affection and intimacy that were little short of disgusting.

It was as if by instinct that between the two of them a binding agreement had been established, to which, before they went to bed, the others in the house also quickly conformed (Tani, the wife, so aged and wasted away! and the three children, Alda, Gilberta and Romano, all of them, as usual, hanging on the lips of their respective consort or parent . . .). The pact proposed by Geremia was the following: that Geo should not even hint indirectly at the political past of his uncle, and he, on his side, should abstain from asking his nephew to recount what he had seen and suffered in that Germany where also he, Geremia Tabet, unless there were proof to the contrary – and this should be remembered also by all those who now thought they might confront him with minor errors in his youth, some only human mistake of political choice made in times so distant as to now seem almost mythical – had himself lost a sister, a brother-in-law and a much-loved nephew. And that was indisputable: the last three years had been terrible. For everyone. Still, things being as they were, a sense of balance and discretion should prevail over every other impulse – the past is past, and it's futile to dig it all up again! Better look to the future. And as to the future, what did it have in store? Geremia had asked at a certain point – assuming the grave but benevolent tone of a paterfamilias who can look into the distance and make out many things there – what kind of plans did Geo himself have? If he was considering, just to suppose, reopening his father's business – a most noble aspiration that he personally could only approve of, and it was worth remembering the Via Vignatagliata warehouse, *that at least*, was still there – then all to the good. Of course he wouldn't fail to help secure the indispensable support of some bank or other. But apart from this, if in the meantime, since the Via Campofranco house was still occupied by the 'Reds', Geo wanted to stay for a while there with them, they could always, no trouble at all, find a place to set up a camp bed.

It was right then, at the words 'camp bed', Daniele Josz recalled, that he had raised his head, focusing all the attention of which he was capable. What was happening? he asked himself. He wanted to understand. He needed to understand.

Streaming with sweat, despite being in pyjamas, Geremia Tabet sat on one side of the big, black dining table, and once more doubtful, perplexed, with the end of his finger worrying at his little pointed grey beard (cut in the classic style of the Fascist squads, which he alone among the old Fascists of Ferrara had had the temerity, the untimeliness or perhaps, who knows, even the shrewdness, to conserve in its proper dimensions). It was on that grey pointed beard and that fat hand which prodded it, that Geo, while he smilingly declined the offer with a shake of his head, fixed his blue eyes with a fanatical stubbornness.

4.

Autumn came to an end. Winter arrived, the long, cold winter that we're used to in these parts. Then spring returned. And slowly, along with the turning of the seasons, the past also returned.

I don't know how believable what I am about to relate will be. It's true that, not so long after, things occurred that would have induced one to imagine that a secret, dynamic relation existed between Geo Josz and Ferrara. Let me explain. Very gradually he grew thin, dried out, by slow steps resuming, apart from the sparse white hair of an absolute silvery whiteness, a face which his hairless cheeks rendered still more youthful, truly like a boy's. But after the removal of the highest piles of rubble and an initial mania of superficial change had exhausted itself, little by little the city, too, began to reassume its old form of sleepy decrepitude which the centuries of clerical decadence that succeeded the distant, fierce and glorious times of Ghibelline rule had turned into an immutable mask. In short, everything rolled on and kept going. Geo, on one side, Ferrara and its society (not excluding those Jews who had escaped the massacre) on the other: each of them was suddenly involved in a vast, ineluctable, fatal flurry of activity. In concordance like two spheres attached by gears and spinning in a single, invisible orbit, which nothing could resist, or halt.

Then came May.

So was it just for this? someone smilingly asked. Was it just so that Geo's blind regret for his lost adolescence should not seem quite so blind, that from the first days of the month linked rows of beautiful girls began once again slowly and gracefully to peddle back from their trips to the surrounding countryside by many routes to the centre of town, their handlebars overflowing with wild flowers? And besides, wasn't it for the same reason that, disgorged from who knows what hiding-place to lean his back against the marble half-column which had kept upright one of the three gates to the Ghetto for centuries, the famous Count Scocca, like a little stone idol, had returned to his spot right at the corner of Via Vignatagliata and Via Mazzini?

And since, one late afternoon around the 15th of the month, a numerous line of young cyclists had almost finished their slow and graceful ascent of Via Mazzini itself, and were about to flow into the Piazza delle Erbe and beyond, laughing – before such a spectacle, always new and always the same, no one could surely begrudge the fact that at this point he should be unwilling to abandon his station. The little stage of Via Mazzini presented on one side, against the sunlight, the serried and luminous ranks of cycling girls, and on the opposite side, grey as the ancient stonework against which he was leaning, Count Lionello Scocca. Well, everyone thought, why should one not be moved by the concrete manifestation of such an allegory, sagely and suddenly harmonizing everything: an anguished, atrocious yesterday, with a today so serene and full of promise? What's certain is that suddenly noticing the penniless old patrician resume, as though nothing had happened, one of his once customary vantage points, one from which someone with good eyesight and subtle hearing could scan the whole of Via Mazzini from top to bottom, it wouldn't have crossed anyone's mind to reproach him for having been a paid informer of the *Organizzazione per la Vigilanza e la Repressione dell'Antifascismo*[8] for years, or having been from 1939 to 1943 the director of the civilian section of the Italo-German Institute of Culture. Even not taking account of the unmistakable, steeply tilted, dull-yellow straw hat, the toothpick gripped between thin lips, the big, sensual nose raised to sniff the reek of rubble that the evening breeze brought with it, that black, visibly re-tinted Hitler moustache might now only inspire sympathetic, even grateful reflections.

So it seemed scandalous that with regard to Count Scocca, all told just a harmless old relic, Geo Josz should behave in a manner that one had to consider alien to any basic sense of decency or discretion: the shock and embarrassment it caused were even more difficult to take precisely because of him, Geo, and all his eccentricities, including his aversion to the so-called 'wartime beards', which for a good while it had become the fashion to smile at with benevolence and understanding, and, by the same standard, to recognize a certain appropriateness that the faces of many gentlemen should now finally dare once more to show themselves in the light of day. And on this topic it was true, true as can be, reasoned one of the better informed, that the lawyer Geremia Tabet, Geo's maternal uncle, had not cut off his beard and perhaps never would. But Good Lord, a poor creature like him! He also deserved a bit of understanding! It wouldn't be that hard. Enough to make the connection between that pathetic, grey, pointed beard and the black Fascist jacket, the

---

8 *OVRA* – the Organization for Vigilance and Repression of Anti-Fascism – was a Fascist organization involved in surveillance.

shiny high, black boots, the black felt fez which for years and years that fine professional had always displayed when he would turn up between midday and one o'clock every Sunday at the Caffè della Borsa, and whoever there was that might want to make a fuss about that would soon lose the courage to say a word.

From the beginning, what happened seemed impossible. No one could believe it. They just couldn't imagine a scene in which Geo, who entered with his usual padded steps into Count Scocca's field of vision as he stood at the corner of Via Vignatagliata, then, with a sudden bestial fury, delivered to the parchment cheeks of that old, resuscitated carrion two dry, really hard slaps, more worthy of a Fascist trooper of Balbo and his companions' times, as someone made explicit, rather than of a survivor of the German gas chambers. In any case, it really happened – dozens of people saw it. But on the other hand, wasn't it odd that, straight away, different and contrasting accounts as to exactly what had happened should have circulated? It made one almost doubt, not only the basis of each of these accounts but even the real, objective event itself, that same double slap, so full and resounding, according to general opinion, as to be heard for almost the entire length of Via Mazzini, from the corner of Piazza delle Erbe, down there at the end, as far at least as the Jewish Temple.

For many, Geo's gesture remained unprovoked and inexplicable.

A little before, he had been seen walking in the same direction as the girls on bicycles, letting himself be slowly overtaken by this procession and never once turning away from the street, his gaze full of stupefaction and joy. Having thus arrived in front of Count Scocca, and abruptly detaching his gaze from a trio of cyclists who had then come parallel with the Oratory of San Crispino, Geo stood stock still, as if the presence of the count, in that place and at that moment, seemed inconceivable to him. His halt, in any case, lasted no more than a second or two, the time required to knit his eyebrows, clench his lips and teeth, convulsively ball up his hands and mutter some words without sense. After which, as though released by a spring, Geo literally leapt on the poor count, who, until that moment, had showed no sign at all of having noticed him.

Is that the whole story? And yet there had been a motive, others objected, and a good one at that! Agreed, Count Scocca might not have been aware of Geo's arrival. Even if rather strange, that couldn't at all be discounted. But as for Geo, however, how was it possible to believe that just at the moment in which the three girls he was gazing fixedly at were about to disappear into the golden haze of Piazza delle Erbe, he had had the time or even the desire to notice the count?

According to these last, instead of merely observing the already almost vesperal scene, with no other concern than to immerse himself in the vague sense of how much the city and he were in perfect harmony, the count had actually done something provocative. And this something, which no one who was passing at a distance of more than a couple of yards could have possibly observed – for the good reason, among other things, that despite everything, the eternal toothpick continued to shift from one to the other corner of his mouth – this something consisted in a subtle sibilance, so weak as to seem shyly casual, an idle little fortuitous whistle, in short, which would surely have remained unnoticed if the tune it hinted at had been anything other than that of 'Lili Marlene':

> Underneath the lantern by the barrack-gate ...

the Count whistled softly but clearly, his own gaze also, despite his seventy or more years, fixed rapturously on the cycling girls. Who can say? Perhaps having stopped his whistling for a moment, he had joined his own voice to the unanimous chorus that rippled along the pavement of Via Mazzini, murmuring in dialect, 'Praised be the Lord for these beauties!' or even, 'Bless you all and the busty saint who protects you!' But what good did it do him? Fortune decreed that that lazy, innocent whistling – innocent, you understand, to anyone else except Geo – should rise to his lips just a fraction too soon. And the outcome for him was those two slaps.

There existed a third version, however, and the third, like the first, didn't mention either 'Lili Marlene' or any other whistling, whether more or less innocent or provocative.

According to this last interpretation, it had been the count who stopped Geo. 'Ah ha!' he had said, under his breath, when he saw him so close. Geo had immediately halted. Then the count had engaged him in conversation, hitting the bull's-eye first time by announcing his full name: 'Look who it isn't!' he had said. 'Could it really be Ruggero Josz, the eldest son of poor Angiolino?' For Lionello Scocca knew everything about Ferrara, and the nearly two years he had had to spend in hiding around Piacenza, just the other side of the river Po, under a false name, had not in the least clouded his memory or weakened his famous ability to recognize at a single glance one face in a thousand. And so, well before Geo had leapt on him and given him those violent slaps, for some minutes they had kept on talking calmly, the count interrogating Geo about his father, for whom, he had said, he *always* had the greatest affection, gathering the most detailed information about the fate of the rest of his family, including Pietruccio, and congratulating Geo on having survived it all; with Geo, on his side, replying sometimes a little awkwardly or reluctantly, it's true, but nevertheless replying. In conclusion, they seemed no different at all from a couple of townsfolk lingering on the pavement to talk of this and that, waiting for darkness to fall. And yet the slaps still needed to be explained. How the devil had they come about? In the opinion of those who gave this account, and who never tired of returning to the theme with the most various of analyses and surmises, it was this that revealed quite what a bizarre character Geo was; it was this that showed just what an 'enigma' he was.

5.

However it actually happened, what's certain is that after that evening in May everything changed. Whoever wished to understand, understood. The others, the majority, at least realized that something serious and irreparable had occurred, the consequences of which could not now be avoided. They had to be put up with.

It was the day after, for example, that people truly saw just how thin Geo had become during this period.

An absurd scarecrow – to the general wonder, unease and alarm, he reappeared dressed in the same clothes he had worn when he'd returned from Germany the preceding August, including the fur cap and the leather jacket. Now they fitted him so loosely – it was clear he hadn't made the least effort to take them in – that they seemed to be draped on a clothes hanger. People saw him coming up the Corso Giovecca in the morning sun which gaily and peacefully shone down upon his rags, and couldn't believe their eyes. So that was how he really was! they thought. In the last months he'd done nothing but grow thinner and thinner, bit by bit, till he was nothing but skin and bones! But no one could raise a laugh. To see him crossing the Giovecca at the City Theatre, then taking the Corso Roma (he had crossed the road as fearful of the cars and bicycles as an old man . . .), there were very few of them who didn't feel themselves inwardly shudder.

And so, from that morning on, without changing his style of dress again, Geo installed himself, one might say, as a fixture at the Caffè della Borsa in Corso Roma, where even if the general, already fading condemnation of the Black Brigade's recent torturers and assassins still held them at bay, still kept them in hiding, the old club-wielding dispensers of castor-oil purges from 1922 and '24, which the last war had somewhat cast into oblivion, began to show themselves again one by one. Clad in rags, Geo stared from his table at the little group of these latter figures with an air between challenge and imploration, and his behaviour contrasted, to his disadvantage as you can guess, with the timidity, the evident desire not to draw too much attention to themselves which these ex-despots expressed with every gesture. By now old, innocuous, with the signs of wreckage that the years of misfortune had stamped chiefly on their faces, and yet still reserved, well mannered, properly dressed, these latter persons displayed a demeanour that was a great deal more human, more decent, and more deserving of sympathy, even. So what after all did Geo Josz really want? a great many people once again began to ask, all of them in agreement that the period immediately after the war, which was so propitious for an examination of both the private and collective conscience, was now over, and this was a luxury that could no longer be afforded. It was the same old question,

Within the Walls

but framed with the brutal impatience that life, imperious in its demands, at this point unambiguously reasserted.

For these reasons, with the exception of Uncle Daniele, who was always brimming with indignation and a polemical impulse at the 'conspicuous' presence at those same tables of some of the most renowned of Ferrara's earliest Fascist squads, it became increasingly rare that any of the habitués of Caffè della Borsa would be prepared to lift themselves off their seats, cross the few intervening yards and then sit down beside Geo.

And that's not to take into account the unease which rewarded those few for their willing efforts of sociability – each time they felt an anxiety flecked with annoyance which they were unable to shrug off for at least two or three days. Frankly, it wasn't possible, they would exclaim, to keep a conversation going with someone dressed so ludicrously! And besides, letting him speak, they would continue, meant that, sure enough, he'd again start telling about Fossoli, Germany, Buchenwald, the fate of his whole family and so on, so that it was impossible to know how to extract themselves. At the caffè, under the awning pummelled by the sirocco blowing across, and as ill-protected as the tables, chairs and the figures reckless enough to sit at them were from the full violence of the afternoon sun, while Geo chattered away unstoppably, there was nothing else to do but follow, from the corner of their eyes, the movements of the builder opposite busy plastering over the holes in the Castle moat's parapet from the bullets left by the execution by firing squad on 15 December 1943. And he, Geo, what was he recounting in the meantime? Without assuming that this was already understood, perhaps he was repeating once again, word for word, the phrases that his father murmured to him before fainting on the path back to the Lager from the salt-mine where both of them were working. Or else, raising his hand in exactly the same way as he had done a hundred times before, he demonstrated the little wave goodbye his mother had given him some twenty minutes after the train had stopped in arrival at the deserted ghostly station in the middle of a forest of fir-trees, as she was pushed away bewildered among a group of women. Or else, with the look of someone about to impart some important news, he again began to tell of Pietruccio, his younger brother, seated next to him in the complete darkness of the lorry that was conveying them from the station to the barracks, and who suddenly disappeared without a complaint or a cry, for ever . . . Horrible, of course, devastating. Still, there was no need to be hoodwinked, those who'd survived such protracted and depressing encounters would declare – you could tell how forced and exaggerated, in short, how false, these stories of Geo's were. And then what a bore! they would add, puffing. Such things had been heard so many times that to have them administered once again (and by the same person as well!) when the Castle clock up there was ringing out hour after hour, one was frankly inclined to give up the ghost and make a run for it. No, let's be clear, you'd need more than a leather jacket and a fur cap to help you swallow this kind of stale swill.

During the remaining months of 1946, the whole of '47 and a good part of '48, this ever more ragged and desolate figure was unceasingly before the eyes of the whole of Ferrara. In the streets, the squares, the cinemas, the theatres, around the sports fields, at public ceremonies: people would turn their heads and there he would be, indefatigable, always with that shadow of saddened bafflement in his eyes. To start holding forth – that was evidently his purpose. By now there was hardly anyone who didn't keep him at bay, who didn't flee him like the plague.

They continued to speak about him, that much, yes.

Having returned from Buchenwald, as the nastier kind of gossip could be overheard claiming, it made sense that he'd choose to stay at home or, if he went out, that he'd prefer plodding down the shadowy narrow ways such as Via Mazzini, Via Vittoria, Via Vignatagliata and Via delle Volte to the broad streets of the Giovecca and Corso Roma. When he once more brought out his lugubrious deportee's uniform, without ever again wearing the fine olive-coloured gabardine which Squarcia, undoubtedly the best tailor in the city, had cut to his exact measure, and then contrived to turn up wherever people were gathered to enjoy themselves or simply with the healthy desire to be together, what possible excuse could one find for such eccentric and offensive behaviour?

Within the Walls

From this perspective, they would continue, the scandal which happened at Club Doro in August 1946 (more than a year, it should be noted, after the end of the war), where, at its opening night Geo had the bright idea of turning up dressed in the same fashion, could stand as an apt example.

Nothing could be said against the place in itself. There was no other way to describe it than with a single word: magnificent. Conceived according to the most modern criteria, it was impossible to criticize, except for the fact that it had been constructed at about a hundred metres from the place where in 1944 the five members of the underground *Comitato di Liberazione Nazionale* had been executed by firing squad – this last detail without doubt rather unpleasant, as the young Bottecchiari, if one looked at the thing from his personal point of view, was perhaps not wrong to underline in the short, satirical article published by him in the *Gazzetta del Po* a couple of days after the opening. At any rate, only the mind of a madman like Geo could have conceived of an idea to sabotage a place which was so happy and convivial in that manner. What harm was there in it? If people now, as it would soon enough be clear, felt the need for a locale outside the walls, and somewhere no one would stop them enjoying themselves, somewhere that, immediately after leaving the cinema, it would be possible to go to, not only to have a snack, but also to dance to the sound of the radio-gramophone among groups of friends and lorry drivers in transit, to stay out even sometimes till dawn – well, didn't people have the right to that? Deranged by the war, and anxious to help on its way the much predicted and wished-for reconstruction, society needed to let its hair down occasionally. Thanks be to God, life had begun again. And when it begins, as one knows, it doesn't look back.

Suddenly faces that had until then expressed doubt and uncertainty now became bitterly questioning, lit up with malice. And what if the camouflage and self-exhibition of Geo, so insistent, and so irritating, had had a precise political intention? What if – and here they winked – with the passing of time he'd become a Commie?

That evening at the dance club, as soon as he came in, he began to show photographs of the members of his family who had died in

Germany to left and right, reaching such a stage of petulance that he was trying to stop the boys and girls from moving off by grabbing hold of their clothes, and they, in that moment, as the radio had suddenly started madly up again, had to brush him off so as to get back on to the dance floor. These were not inventions at all, a great many of the most reliable people had been witnesses to the fact. So what else had Geo been referring to with those gestures of his, with those demented antics, with that bizarre and macabre pantomime, seasoned with his saccharine grins and half-imploring, half-menacing grimaces, unless it was that he and Nino Bottecchiari, having finally reached an agreement about the house in Via Campofranco, were now in bed together and in total agreement *also about everything else, which is to say politics, which is to say communism*? But then, if he had accepted the role of useful idiot, wasn't it more than justified that the Friends of America Club, which in all the chaos and enthusiasm of the immediate post-war period had thought it opportune to enroll Geo too as one of their board members, had then, with due care, decided to cancel him from the list? Let's be clear about this: it's likely that no one would have dreamt of chucking him out, if it hadn't been he first of all that *wanted* the scandal and the moderate sanctions against him that followed. No, this was far from being nonsense! The proof could be seen that other famous night – it happened in February 1947 – when he showed up at the door of the club dressed as a beggar and with his head shaved like a convict: truly reduced to a human wreck – that's the word – the spitting image of the famous tramp, Tugnìn da la Ca' di Dio – there, in the vestibule full of coats and furs, he had started to bawl that they should let him through, since whoever was enrolled and had paid their fees had the right to frequent the club how and when they wanted. Expelling someone is always unpleasant. Of course it is. Besides, wasn't it true that for quite a while, to be exact, from the autumn of the year before, the board of directors of the Friends of America Club had voted unanimously to return as soon as possible to their old title of the Union Club, once again reducing the enrolled membership to the aristocratic families of the Costabilis, the Del Sales, the Maffeis, the Scroffas, the Scoccas, etc., as well as the more select sector of bourgeoisie drawn from the liberal professions and landowners – Catholic, but in certain exceptional cases, also Jewish? Like a swollen river that had broken its banks and hugely flooded the surrounding countryside, the world now needed to return to its original margins: that was the point. This explained, among other things, why even old Maria, Maria Ludargnani, who during the same winter had reopened her house of assignation in Via Arianuova – in just a few weeks, it became clear that this was the only, in some way public, place where it was still possible to gather and meet together without political or even apolitical opinion continually leaping out to poison all relations, and the evenings spent there, mainly chatting or playing gin rummy with the girls, were a reminder of the blessed times before the great upheaval – why even she had thought it necessary, that other time Geo had come to knock on her door, to tell him roundly and clearly, *Nix*, to go away, and in the end declaring in dialect, after making very sure with her eye to the spyhole that he'd been swallowed up again by the mist: '*Agh mancava sol ach gnéss déntar anch clucalà!*'[9] In conclusion: if no one had dreamt that Maria Ludargnani, prohibiting Geo's entry to her 'house', had defrauded him of some right, then one had to admit that the Union Club had acted towards him in a manner that was most proper, astute and responsible. And then just think about it! If you can't exclude whomever you want from your own house, where is freedom, what sense is there in talking about democracy?

Only in 1948, after the 18 April elections, after the local *ANPI* section was forced to transfer to the three rooms in the ex-Fascist HQ in Viale Cavour – and with this the belated proof was given that the rumour of 'adhesion' to the Communist Party of the Via Campofranco house's owner was pure fantasy – only in the summer of that year did Geo Josz finally decide to abandon the game. Exactly like a character in a novel, he disappeared without warning, without leaving the slightest trace behind. At once some said he had emigrated to Palestine in the wake of Dr Herzen, others claimed he'd gone to South America, yet others to some undefined 'country beyond the Iron Curtain', and others still that he had drowned

---

9 In Ferrarese dialect: 'Just what we need – for that one there to be in here!'

himself in the Po, throwing himself at night from the height of the iron bridge of Pontelagoscuro which had been recently reconstructed.

This topic continued to crop up for the next few months: at the Caffè della Borsa, at the Doro, in Maria Ludargnani's house of assignation, everywhere, to some extent. Daniele Josz was offered on more than one occasion the opportunity to hold a public enquiry. The lawyer Geremia Tabet also intervened to represent questions concerning the inheritance of his nephew. In the meantime: 'What a madman!' was heard again and again.

They would shake their heads benignly, tighten their lips in silence, raise their eyes to the heavens.

'If he'd only had a bit of patience!' they'd add, sighing, and they were now, once again, sincere, once again sincerely regretful on his behalf.

Then they would say that as time heals everything in this world, and thanks to which Ferrara itself was rising from the ruins the same as it had once been, so time would in the end have brought some peace even to him, would have helped him return to a normal life, in short, to re-establish him within the city. And yet instead the opposite had happened. He had preferred to go away. Disappear. Even to kill himself. To play the tragic hero. Exactly at this point when, renting out the big house on Via Campofranco and giving the right boost to his father's firm, he would have been able to live very comfortably, like a gentleman, and to consider among other things making a new family for himself. But no, let's be honest: they really had treated him with more than enough patience. The episode with Count Scocca, without even cataloguing the rest, should in the end be enough to reveal that, to see what kind of an eccentric he was, what sort of living enigma had landed among them . . .

6.

An enigma, that's it.

And yet, in the absence of any more certain clues, if we consider that sense of the absurd, and at the same time that of revelatory truth, which any encounter can have just as dusk is falling, the episode with Count Scocca shouldn't have seemed so enigmatic, shouldn't have been anything that could not have been understood by a heart that felt a little solidarity.

It's true that daylight is boredom, a hard sleep for the spirit, 'tedious mirth', as the Poet says. But in the end let the hour of dusk arrive, the hour equally woven of shadow and light of a peaceful dusk in May, and then note how the things and people that before had appeared utterly normal and indifferent can suddenly show themselves as they truly are: it can happen that all at once – and then it is as though you've been struck by lightning – they speak for the first time of themselves and of you.

'What am I doing here with this person? Who is this person? And I, replying to his questions, playing along with him, who on earth am I?'

Two slaps, after some moments of mute bewilderment, had been the thunderous reply to the insistent, albeit polite questions of Lionello Scocca. But to those questions there might well have been the alternative reply of a furious, inhuman cry – so loud that the whole city, as much of it as was still remaining beyond the deceptively intact scene of Via Mazzini, and as far off as the distant, breached walls, would have heard it with horror.

The Final Years of Clelia Trotti

I.

To call the vast, architectonic complex of Ferrara's Municipal Cemetery beautiful, so beautiful as even to be consolatory, there'd be the risk, even among us, of provoking the usual sniggers, the superstitious gestures to fend off the evil eye always at the ready in Italy to greet any speech that refers to death without deploring it. All the same, once you arrive at the end of Via Borso d'Este, a perfectly straight little road, with the marble-cutting workshops huddled at the start and the florists at the end, and entirely overwhelmed by the thick foliage of the two big private parks on either side, the unexpected vista of the Piazza della Certosa and of the adjacent cemetery, gives, there's no use denying it, a joyful, almost festive impression.

To have an idea of what the Piazza della Certosa is like, one should think of an open, nearly empty meadow, scattered as it is in the distance with some occasional funerary monuments for illustrious nineteenth-century lay-persons: a kind of parade ground, in short. To the right, the rugged, unfinished facade of the church of San Cristoforo, and also, curving in a wide semi-circle until it reaches the city walls, a red, early-sixteenth-century portico on which some afternoons the sun beats down to magnificent effect; to the left, only small, semi-rustic houses, only the low boundary walls of the big vegetable gardens and orchards of which even now in this most northerly zone of the city there is an abundance, houses and low walls which, in contrast to the opposite side, do not offer the least obstacle to the long rays of afternoon or evening sunlight. In the space between these boundaries there's very little, I repeat, that speaks of death. Even the two pairs of terracotta angels

Within the Walls

right at the top of the portico, awaiting the signal from heaven to blow into the elongated bronze trumpets they've already put to their lips, have nothing about them that could really be considered threatening. They swell their red cheeks, impatient to blow, eager to play: the baroque artist must surely have found the likeness for the faces of these four robust-looking lads in the surrounding Ferrarese countryside.

It may be because of the dreamy sweetness of the place, and also, it should be said, its almost perfect and perpetual solitude, but the fact is that the Piazza della Certosa has always been the favourite site for lovers' trysts. Where would you go in Ferrara, even today, when you want to talk to someone a little away from the world? The first choice is the Piazza della Certosa. There, should things proceed as might be hoped, it would be only too easy to move on later to the nearby bastions, where you can find as many places as you like away from the prying eyes of nursemaids that are so vigilant in the piazza around the hour of dusk. And if, on the contrary, the idyll doesn't proceed, it would be just as easy and, at the same time, without any risk of being compromised, to return from there together towards the city centre. This is a custom that has been established of old, a kind of ritual, probably as ancient as Ferrara itself. It was in force before the war, as it is today and will be tomorrow. True, the bell tower of San Cristoforo, docked halfway up by an English grenade in April 1945 and remaining thus, a sort of bloody stump, is there to declare that any guarantee of permanence is illusory, and therefore that the message of hope that the sunlit porticoes with their reddened heat seem to express is only a lie, a trick, a beautiful deception. Just as the bell tower of San Cristoforo has ceased to exist, without doubt, sooner or later, even the agile procession of arches that stretch like two arms up towards the light will cease to exist, to lull and delude the souls of those who contemplate it. Even this will come to an end sooner or later. As will everything. But in the meanwhile, only a few steps from the thousands and thousands of citizens who lie in row after row of the cemetery sited behind, on the vast grassy expanse scattered here and there with funerary steles and memorial stones, life's peaceful, indifferent bustle goes on unperturbed, refusing to throw in the towel, to give up the ghost; what prophesy would seem more destined to be erased, to remain unheard in the excited atmosphere of the nearing dusk, than one which promises an inevitable, final nothingness?

The atmosphere of general, almost sporting excitement immediately provoked in the Piazza della Certosa by a funeral cortège too different from the usual to pass unobserved, a cortège that one autumn afternoon in 1946 emerged from Via Borso with a big band at its head, couldn't but immediately attract the attention of the habitués of the place – mainly nursemaids, children and enamoured couples, inducing the first, seated on the grass beside prams, to raise bewildered eyes from the newspaper or their sewing, the second to stop running after or playing with balls and the last to release their clasped hands and quickly draw back from each other.

The autumn of 1946. The war now over. And yet the first impression, observing the funeral which in that moment was making its entry into Piazza della Certosa, was to have been transported back to May or June of the previous year, to the fiery period of the Liberation. With a sudden leap of the heart and the blood, it was like once again being called on to witness one of those then typical and frequent examinations of the collective conscience by which an old, guilty society desperately tries to renew itself. No sooner had one noticed the thicket of red flags which followed the coffin, and the scores of placards inscribed with an assortment of slogans: ETERNAL GLORY TO CLELIA TROTTI or ALL HONOUR TO CLELIA TROTTI, SOCIALIST MARTYR or VIVA CLELIA TROTTI HEROIC EXAMPLE TO THE WORKING CLASS etc., and the bearded partisans who carried them aloft, and above all the absence in front of the carriage of priests and clergymen, than one's gaze hurried ahead to where the procession was making its way: a grave, that is, dug in the portion of the cemetery exactly in front of the main entrance to the church of San Cristoforo where, apart from an English protestant who had died from malaria in 1917, no one had been buried for more than fifty years.

And yet, returning to the funeral cortège, the head of which was

Within the Walls

by now only tens of metres from the humble, secular grave which was waiting open – another crowd in the meantime was unceasingly pouring out from Via Borso – even a slightly trained eye would quickly be aware, from innumerable details, how deceptive was that initial impression of a magical return to the atmosphere of 1945.

Let's take, for example, the band. It's worth specifying that it proceeded in front of, but was detached from, the carriage, and played Chopin's funeral march in slow time. The brand-new uniforms worn by the band members, one of the boasts of the Communist administration only recently installed in the municipality, would undoubtedly have enchanted a foreigner, an uninformed newcomer, but not someone who, underneath the large caps with shiny visors in the style of the American police, was able to trace one by one the good-natured and dejected features of the Orfeonica's old zealots, dispersed who knows where, poor devils, at the time of the shootings and ambushes that followed the break-up of the Front and the popular uprising. But the punctilious staging, so alien to the genial chaos typical of revolutions, was if possible even more evident in the compact formation of some fifteen *arzdóre* from the Po delta who, carrying in pairs great wreaths of carnations and roses, surrounded the funeral carriage on all sides like a guard of honour. To see the earthy faces, deeply marked with fatigue, of these mature female heads of the family, all roughly the same age as Clelia Trotti, would be enough to be able to guess where they had come from and how they had arrived. Gathered together at Ferrara from the furthest villages of the Adriatic coast, at midday in the city they will certainly have found someone to offer them the refreshment of *pastasciutta*, a slice of roast beef and a quart of wine, but not the chance of a much-needed rest. The same bureaucratic mind that had provided a table adorned with red paper flags had then inflexibly decided that after the meal these ancient female farm labourers should clean themselves as best they could from their dusty journey and then put on, over their everyday clothes, a strange kind of tunic: red, naturally, and peppered with lots of tiny black hammers and sickles. Thus clad, they now appeared as it had been decreed that they should – almost like priestesses of socialism. But their heavy, bewildered steps, the wild stares which they cast about, gave them away only too clearly. It made one think that the laborious odyssey which, from the start of the day, they had already undertaken was sadly very far from being over. Shedding those tunics some hours later, then getting back into the same three or four cars that had transported them into the city, they would finally be restored to their impoverished dwellings only late at night. And who knows if before letting them depart anyone might remember to sit them down for a second around the table adorned with flags?

Immediately behind the funeral carriage, the authorities followed in several lines that filled the small space between the carriage itself and the undifferentiated crowd carrying flags and placards.

These were Socialists, Communists, Catholics, Liberals, activists, *Repubblicani-storici*[10]: in short, the complete ex-directory of the last secret *Comitato di Liberazione Nazionale*, reconstructed with all its members for the occasion. Added to and mixed in with this group, one noticed some other figures who were not, strictly speaking, political, such as the engineer Cohen, president of the Jewish community, and the newly nominated mayoress, Dr Bettitoni.

So, even if the honourable Mauro Bottecchiari, usually known in Ferrara as 'the prince of our forum', couldn't call himself the city's most representative political figure after the recent administrative elections had seen the crushing victory of the Communists, it was to him, to his uncombed, silver head of hair, to his high-coloured, loyal, convivial face that everyone's gaze first turned. It's true that on the actual political plane, at this point, the honourable Bottecchiari signified pretty well nothing ('A reformist à la Turati!' people on the Communist side had begun to call him). But compared to the old lion, what an insipid figure the other members of the ex-directory of the final underground *Comitato di Liberazione Nazionale* cut! Apart from Dr Herzen, the so-called prefect of the Liberation, recently emigrated to Palestine, no one else was missing. There was the lawyer Galassi-Tarabini of the Democratic Christian Party, who,

---

10 A political party of the centre, but anti–Fascist. For information about the *Comitato*, see footnote on p. 67.

Within the Walls

worried to find himself there at a purely secular, civic funeral – and for this reason he swivelled every which way his washed-out blue eyes that seemed always about to fill with tears – walked beside Don Bedogni, of the Catholic Action Party, who, on the contrary, in a French beret and baggy trousers, even in these circumstances made an effort to display the consummate ease, the unprejudiced, modern suavity which, in the post-war period, made him one of the most renowned public figures of the entire Emilia Romagna. There was the engineer Sears, of the *Partito d'Azione*,[11] who, as usual, walked a little apart from the others with his small hands clasped behind his back, and was smiling slightly to himself. There was the little group of *Repubblicani-storici* – the chemist Riccoboni, the tailor Squarcia, the dentist Canella – rather embarrassed, you could clearly see, but still willing to keep up with the times. And finally there was Alfio Mori, the federal Communist of Ferrara: small, dark, bespectacled, with the hint of a smile that revealed his big white upper canines, he advanced in quiet conversation with Nino Bottecchiari, the young, promising provincial secretary of the *Associazione Nazionale Partigiani d'Italia*.[12] And yet, walking stooped and meek, reduced in appearance to a little band of nobodies, over all of them the honourable Bottecchiari enjoyed the easiest of victories. Seeing him looming over them by a head and continuously turning about that same red, ireful face before which even Sciagura, the notorious Sciagura, sent to attack him on the crowded Corso Giovecca in the remote year of 1922, had been forced to beat an ignominious retreat, there was no doubt that he, the lawyer, the honourable Mauro Bottecchiari, was back again, if only for a day, the indisputable, acknowledged leader of Ferrara's anti-Fascists. So nothing could be more natural, after the carriage had stopped beside the grave, and the *arzdóre* of the Po delta had slid out from it the zinc coffin of Clelia Trotti, than that it should be he, the honourable Bottecchiari, who should be the first to move towards the cata-

11 The Action Party was a radical Socialist party formed in 1942 and dissolved in 1947. It had adopted the name of Guiseppe Mazzini's democratic party from nearly a century before.
12 For the *ANPI*, see footnote on p. 69.

falque. The solemn transferral of the remains of Clelia Trotti, who had died three years before in the prison of Codigoro, during the German occupation, from the Codigoro graveyard to the Communal Cemetery of Ferrara, could not possibly have exempted him from the role of absolute eminence that was his due. It was his responsibility as Clelia Trotti's oldest comrade in the Socialist struggle to open the series of commemorative speeches.

'Comrades!' shouted the honourable Bottecchiari – a raucous, imperious cry which echoed far along under the cemetery's porticoes.

'Comrades,' he added in a lower tone, after a pause, as if he were preparing to go full tilt.

He then began to speak, gesticulating. And his words would most certainly have reached the furthest corners of the Piazza della Certosa – the face of the honourable gentleman had at once become purple with the effort – if at that very moment a motor scooter in Via Borso hadn't revved up explosively: a Vespa, one of the first to be seen coursing about the city just after the end of the war. The silencer on the Vespa's exhaust pipe was missing. Missing? More than that, the showy chrome metal contraption which stuck out below, on the left-hand side of the scooter, served the opposite purpose: not to suppress the motor's chugging revs but to make them drier and more obstreperous, better suited to the restless adolescent hand that twitched continuously to release them.

Interrupted in his oratorical flourish, the honourable Bottecchiari became silent. Contracting his white, bushy eyebrows, he directed his gaze towards the end of the square. He was short-sighted and, not seeing clearly, with a nervous gesture of his big hand that always trembled, took out a tiny pince-nez. The distant image of a young girl on a Vespa – who, having left Via Borsa but now slowing down, was riding along the portico arches of the cemetery behind the mass of persons in a semicircle – soon came into focus. Oh, it must be a very young girl, from a good family, the honourable Bottecchiari said, twisting his lips in a grimace of sadness. Who could she be, whose child? he added, with a reticent but irritated expression, as if he were going over in his mind all the names of the most well-off families of the city's bourgeoisie, among whom the Bottecchiaris were also numbered, as if surveying one by one all those sturdy, tanned, teenage legs which at least two months of swimming at Rimini, Riccione and so on, had pared down – oh yes, the bourgeoisie, after the storm of the war has passed, quickly resume all their old habits! 'What a lack of decency!' he preached at them, loudly: with the bitterness of one who feels wounded, misunderstood. 'I wonder,' he added, pointing with outstretched hand at the very young scooterist, upright in her saddle down there, the slight, almost masculine torso clad in a black silk shirt and with a red ribbon in her hair, 'I wonder if one can be much more disrespectful than that!' And the crowd, hundreds of scandalized faces, turned all together to make a hushing hiss.

'Ssh!'

The girl didn't understand, or else didn't care to. Although she had by now reached that part of the square she was heading for – the honourable Bottecchiari, who had seen her disappear behind a high barrier of people hoisted up on to the kerb-posts around the churchyard the better to witness the ceremony, had waited in vain for her to reappear into the open further on – she not only didn't feel inclined to turn off the engine, but instead, unabashed, every now and then kept up her game of sudden, clamorous revvings.

'For God's sake, get her to stop!' cried the honourable Bottecchiari in exasperation.

'Ssh!' repeated an energetic chorus of the men who had climbed on to the kerb-posts: necks that turned, eyes that from above could admonishingly survey a scene that he, Bottecchiari, even on tiptoe, was completely unable to observe. And yet, in the meantime, no one who wanted to put an end to that scandal was prepared to get down, and thereby risk losing their place!

Seated on the stone border of the churchyard, in a good spot to see everything – the honourable Bottecchiari over there, waiting to be able to resume his eulogy, and here, two or three metres away from him, the girl on the Vespa whose blue eyes just in that moment caught his own – Bruno Lattes gave a start.

He felt uneasy (what follows in this story will explain why) and lowered his head. When, after a few seconds he raised it again, the girl was already looking elsewhere. She was now staring, in a clearly ironic way, at a boy more or less her own age, as ashen-blond as herself and with the same hard, indifferent look in his bright blue irises. A tennis racket between his legs, and a white pullover tied by its sleeves around his neck, the boy was just in front of her, likewise seated on the churchyard border. The two, it was clear to Bruno Lattes, were going out together – and for that reason had arranged to meet here – in the Piazza della Certosa, of course! But who was she, who were her parents? Bruno kept thinking, suddenly, spasmodically attracted to her, to the red ribbon that tied up the girl's hair. Was it possible that the war, the years in which he had been a boy and she a child, had left not the tiniest trace on her? Was it possible that everywhere in Italy the adolescents could be like this, as if, unaware of anything, they had been born teenagers from out of the pages of an illustrated American magazine?

'I've been waiting for you for half an hour,' said the young tennis player, without giving any sign of meaning to get up.

'And *you're* complaining!' replied the girl.

She nodded, with a little sneer at the square teeming with people.

'Looks to me like you've found something to keep you happy.'

'Ssh! Be quiet!' repeated for the third time the men perched on the posts.

The boy assumed the hard look of a gangster from the movies. With a grin he pointed at the scooter.

'Why not give that little twitchy hand of yours a rest?'

'I'd prefer to go somewhere else,' the girl grumbled, though, in the meantime having got down from the saddle and switched off the motor, she had sat down beside her friend. 'What d'you want to do? Stick around here?'

'Before this coffin that carries the mortal remains of Clelia Trotti, of our unforgettable Clelia,' the honourable Bottecchiari had resumed in a tone of voice which foreshadowed the big tears which would soon begin to roll down his apoplectic cheeks, 'comrades, friends, fellow citizens all, I cannot but immediately recall the past we have lived through together. If I'm not mistaken, we came to know each other, Clelia Trotti, and I who address you, in the April of 1904...'

Bruno Lattes slowly turned to look in the direction of the speaker. But once again he gave a start. The little man, dressed all in black, straight as a ramrod, who stood down there at the side of the honourable Bottecchiari – didn't he know him? Could he be Cesare Rovigatti, the shoemaker of Piazza Santa Maria in Vado?

How little time has passed, he thought to himself with regret, since he, after 25 July 1943, had left Ferrara in August for Rome, and then no more than a year after, for the United States of America! And yet how much had happened in such a short time!

At the start of those last, atrocious three years, his parents, who never believed they would have to flee, never saw the need to provide themselves with false papers, were taken away by the Germans, and both their names now figured among the nearly two hundred others on the memorial stone which the Jewish community had had fixed on the facade of the Temple in Via Mazzini. And he? He, on the contrary, had escaped from Ferrara. He got away at the right moment not to suffer the same fate as his mother and father, or alternatively not to have been shot by firing squad in the following December at the time of the Salò Republic, with the reward, apart from having saved his skin, of being by now on his way towards a tranquil, dignified university career: he was so far only a lecturer in Italian, rather than having tenure, but soon he'd be given a permanent post, which would result (after some months of waiting) in his acquiring the longed-for American citizenship...

In short, the last three years seemed like a lifetime. And yet Rovigatti, thank God – Bruno Lattes continued thinking and, without being aware, nodded his head in the affirmative – didn't seem to have aged at all; even his grizzled black hair had remained more or less the same. Likewise the honourable Bottecchiari and all the other Ferrarese anti-Fascists, today assembled in an official plenary for the funeral of Clelia Trotti, whom he had known personally and spent time with from 1939 on. None of them seemed to have aged, nor had Ferrara itself, which, apart from the wreckage caused by the war, which was being speedily repaired, had seemed to him from the first identical to the city of his childhood and adolescence. Although stripped of all its furnishings, even the house he had been born and brought up in had been restored to him intact, intact like an empty shell ... Likewise for Rovigatti – perhaps especially for him! – it seemed as though time had passed in vain, or even come to a halt.

There it all was, preserved in Piazza della Certosa, he concluded his thoughts – the little, old provincial world he'd left behind. Almost like a wax replica: there it all was, exactly the same as itself. But Clelia Trotti?

The last time he'd met her had coincidentally been here, in Piazza della Certosa, nearly in the same spot where her coffin now rested, the day before his departure. In his memory, during the following interminable forty months, Clelia had never changed.

How he would have liked, now, to have found her, too, fixed in wax, motionless like a grotesque statuette that, torn between scorn and compassion, he could position as he pleased! With a smile, he would have told her: 'See, wasn't I telling the truth when I promised I'd return? And you were wrong not to believe me.'

If only she hadn't changed, had remained for ever the same as he had seen her that last afternoon before he went away, before he cut the cord and saved himself. He would have asked this of her, if, in the meantime, she hadn't died.

2.

In the late autumn of 1939, almost a year after the proclamation of the Racial Laws, when he decided to go in search of Clelia Trotti, Bruno Lattes still knew almost nothing about her. From what he had heard, she was a small, withered woman, nearly sixty, who didn't take care of herself, with the look of a nun, who, if you passed her on the street, you wouldn't even notice. On the other hand, who in Ferrara at that time could claim to know her personally, or even remember that she existed? Even the honourable Bottecchiari, despite having acted a bit in his youth, and at the beginning of his political career having directed with her the legendary *Torch of the*

People – they'd even been lovers, according to the whispered gossip, at least until the First World War broke out – even he, at the outset, gave the impression of having completely lost touch with her.

'Here he is, our young Lattes!' the honourable Bottecchiari had cried out from behind the imposing, Renaissance-style table that served him as a desk on the occasion that Bruno had gone to his office hoping to glean some information about the old schoolmistress. 'Do come in! Come in!' he had added heartily, seeing him hesitating at the doorway. 'How's your father?'

Thus saying, he extended his powerful right hand by way of greeting and encouraging him, half-rising from his comfy lawyer's seat upholstered in red satin while looking him up and down with a satisfied expression. And yet, as soon as he heard the name of Trotti, he was ready to withdraw into a state of cautious reticence.

'But yes . . . just a moment . . .' he replied, with obvious embarrassment, 'someone, I can't remember who, must have told me that she's living . . . that's she's gone to stay in the Saraceno district . . . in Via Belfiore . . .'

He then changed the subject to speak of other things: about the war, the Phoney War, the likelihood of Italy's entering the war, or rather 'of Mussolini' doing so, and about Hitler's next possible 'strikes'. 'Oh yes,' could be read in his blue eyes, full of little red veins and lit with triumphant irony, 'oh yes! For twenty years you've looked at me with suspicion, *even you people* have avoided and despised me as an anti-Fascist, as a subversive, an enemy to the regime, and now that *your* lovely regime is chucking you out, here you are, all penitent, with your ears flat and your tail between your legs!'

He spoke of all kinds of other things, while never straying far from matters of international politics and that kind of commentary about things military which, by this stage, when the radio transmitted the daily news of the war halted at the Maginot Line, overflowed even at the Caffè della Borsa. At least on that occasion, Bruno thought, it was clear he didn't want the conversation to stray from this kind of territory. His tone of bland complicity shouldn't mislead anyone who listened to think otherwise. As justification for this, the friendship that he, Bottecchiari, had always had with Bruno's father, also a lawyer, since their long-ago schooldays – rather than friendship it might be better to call it professional consideration between middle-class and well-off colleagues – this tacit understanding had been maintained between the two of them, even after the March on Rome, even after the assassination of Matteotti, by the solemn and confidential greetings they would smilingly exchange in the Corso Giovecca from the distance of one pavement to the other ... So much so that, later, at the end of their 'pleasant pow-wow', as the honourable gentleman had put it, it was a big surprise for Bruno that it was he, Bottecchiari, who, unprompted, just as they were saying their goodbyes, should have returned to the topic of Clelia Trotti.

'If you manage to track her down, do send her my greetings,' he said with a cordial grin, patting Bruno on the back just as he was halfway to the door.

And then, in a lower tone:

'You don't know Rovigatti, do you – Cesare Rovigatti, the shoemaker who has his workshop in Piazza Santa Maria in Vado, beside the church?'

'We always go to him to get our shoes resoled!' The words escaped Bruno and he felt himself blushing. 'Why do you ask?'

'He's someone who'll be able to tell you where Signora Trotti is,' explained the honourable gentleman. 'Go and find him. Ask him. But be careful –' he added (the crack of the frosted-glass door had closed so it was now merely a spyhole) – 'be very careful as she's under surveillance!'

When he was downstairs, hovering at the main entrance, the first thing Bruno did was look up at the faintly lit square face of the clock in the square. It was seven o'clock. Why not go at once to see Rovigatti? If he hurried, he could easily find him still there in his dark little den. He was the kind of person who never closed before eight, eight-thirty.

He waited for the most opportune moment to slip away without drawing any attention to himself. He finally stepped out, and having hurried across the open space in front, as always teeming with people at that hour, he took cover under the Duomo's arches.

He began to walk more slowly now, his hands deep in his raincoat pockets, and at the same time he pondered the ambiguous welcome he'd received from Bottecchiari.

Once again he saw his face as it had last appeared through the half-closed door. He had said 'Rovigatti' and given a wink as he spoke. So, what had he meant, the honourable Bottecchiari, with that meaningful wink? Had he wanted, with that rather vulgar sign and the whispered name, to excuse himself indirectly for having kept their whole conversation a bit on the general side? Or alternatively, had he wanted to hint at the bond that had tied him, and perhaps, who knows, still secretly did, to his old Party comrade, a hint which, it's clear, would take away, even from the little that had been said, any *political* import? In fact this was consistent with the way he usually behaved in Ferrara, when half boastfully, half ashamed of himself, he would confide man to man (but above all to other middle-class persons!) of a relationship he was having with a working-class girl. Exactly in that manner, and from time immemorial. And yet, on the other hand, wasn't it quite odd that the honourable Bottecchiari, an ex-deputy of the Socialist Party, a veteran anti-Fascist, one who gave the impression of never having kowtowed to anyone, should be prepared to adopt – it didn't matter whether for a joke or flirtatiously – the same stupid and cruel sulkiness of the conformist herd which arrogantly occupied the streets, the caffès, the cinemas, the dancing halls, the sports grounds, the barbers' shops, even the brothels, excluding from the *Imperium* whoever was or seemed different? The truth was that not even the honourable Bottecchiari had escaped without being harmed, without his character, the fierce integrity of his youth, being tainted by the pressure of those decades, from 1915 to '39, which had seen in Ferrara, as everywhere else in Italy, the progressive degeneration of every human value. It's true, his fellow lawyers, all of them Fascist in the extreme, literally foamed with anger every time, holding forth in the courthouse, he made it clear what he thought – more than one, without doubt, would have liked to hurl him to the ground, grab him by the folds of his toga, and yell in his face, 'You're trying to insinuate such and such, eh? Admit it!' But in reality they'd always let him hold forth, content in the end to have given the old battler free rein once more to indulge his eternal saying-without-saying, his never-ending, tireless hinting, which over the years had become a kind of tic, an addiction, almost the expression of a second nature. If the honourable Bottecchiari, regardless of his past, was always prepared, when leaving his office or the court on his way home every day, to walk down Corso Giovecca defiantly flaunting his mane of almost luminously white hair in the face of his few friends and many enemies, none of this had happened without his too, at some level, having at least partly forgiven us.

Rapt in these thoughts that held his heart in the grip of anxiety, jostling and being jostled by passers-by, Bruno slowly ascended Via Mazzini and Via Saraceno. 'How disgusting!' he hissed every now and then between his teeth. He looked with hatred at the sparkling shop windows, the people stopped in front of them to look at the goods on display, the shopkeepers that showed themselves in their doorways, more or less the same in their behaviour, he thought to himself, as the shrews who kept watch, always half in, half out of their huddled little houses in Via Colomba, Via Sacca and thereabouts. Still ensnared and enslaved by the passion which, since the August of that year, had tied him to one of the most brilliant and sought-after girls in Ferrara, Adriana Trentini, the women that passed him going the other way and brushed against him without noticing him (the beautiful, the blonde and the elegant especially) seemed to him in their whole way of being at once adorable and detestable, to carry the ill-disguised mark of depravity. 'What trash! What shameful scum!' he kept repeating, not even under his breath.

And yet, gradually as he proceeded, and the streets became narrower and less well-lit, his fury and disgust began to abate. Taking a left turn into Via Borgo di Sotto, he came out almost level with Via Belfiore and was about to cross. But from the closed blinds of the houses in Via Belfiore, at least as far as where the little street made a sharp bend, only a sparse, yellowish light filtered out. Who could he ask, whose doorbell could he ring? By now everyone would be eating supper – at his own home as well, they'd be expecting him. Remembering Rovigatti, he ended up going on.

Within the Walls

Obscured by fog, the Piazza Santa Maria in Vado suddenly cleared before him, revealing the sombre facade of the church on one side, the dark opening of Via Scandiana in front, in the centre the little fountain where a group of women were seated chattering, shabby little workshops and hovels all around, from which emanated, together with a faint light and smells of roast beef and chestnut cake, vague and various sounds: an anvil beaten weakly, a child's muffled sobbing, a 'goodnight' and a 'goodbye' exchanged by two elderly men from deep under an invisible portico, a clinking of glasses . . . His gaze was quickly drawn to the left by a small, slightly better-lit window. Rovigatti was there, seated at his cobbler's workbench. Beyond the steamed-up windowpane his familiar outline could be discerned. And as he made his way towards him, it was as though he stood still and the unchanged image of the shoemaker was coming towards him through the fog.

He went in, took off his hat, offered his hand to Rovigatti above the workbench, sat down in front of him and at once and without any difficulty obtained the full and exact address of the schoolmistress: 36, Via Fondo Banchetto, at the house of Codecà. Then they began to talk. So that evening, as well, when he returned home the supper had been finished long before.

The very next day, he timidly rang the doorbell of 36, Via Fondo Banchetto. And certainly, if he had been invited in at once, if a fat woman with salt-and-pepper hair and a shy manner – 'her sister' as Rovigatti had drily explained – hadn't come to the door to tell him that the schoolmistress was not at home, if she, the same she, in a black satin smock and with the Fascist badge pinned to her breast, hadn't reappeared the next day to tell him that the schoolmistress was giving lessons and therefore couldn't receive any visitors, and the next day again, that she wasn't well, and, yet another day, that she'd gone to Bologna and wouldn't be back before next week, and so on week after week, he wouldn't have had the opportunity to become, as he did in fact become, friends with Rovigatti. He had understood from the first moment that he would be kept waiting at Santa Maria in Vado. But for how long? he had wondered. Had Clelia Trotti come to know him through his attempts to contact her? Had her married sister Codecà told her that he came to the house almost every day?

Each time he pressed the bell his heart would be beating fast, and each time he felt the disappointment anew. Rejected, he would withdraw to Piazza Santa Maria in Vado, not three hundred metres away. He would never find Rovigatti's glass door shut, on that he could rely. He only needed to push it open with two fingers, and there would always be the shoemaker in person, with his tuft of raven hair which still youthfully flopped over to one side of his pale forehead, stippled with blackheads around the temples, with his smile, with his dark, almost feverish eyes which gazed up at him. 'Good evening, Signorino Bruno, how are you?' Rovigatti would say. 'Do come in please and make yourself at home.' And did he not truly do so?

They would sometimes talk till after nine o'clock. In the meantime, seated on the bench facing him, Bruno would watch the shoemaker at work.

Rolling the pack thread in palms as tough as the leather he had cut out in the shape of a sole, Rovigatti drew the needle back and forth with a measured energy. He perennially kept a handful of tacks in his mouth, and his lips and tongue were wonders of precision and promptness in disgorging them one by one into the light as the occasion required. Gripping a shoe tightly between his knees, he hammered the tacks in tirelessly and automatically ... How skilled and assured he was! Bruno thought. What strength and self-awareness he seems able to derive from manual labour! Making busy with his big, blackened, incredibly calloused hands didn't seem in the least to impede his conversation. Rather the opposite. A tack hammered home through the thickness of leather with a single stroke seemed sometimes to serve his purposes better than any argument.

And yet what was it that still kept them apart? he often asked himself. What stopped him from winning the shoemaker's full and absolute confidence? Class difference, perhaps? Could it really be that?

Speaking ill of Fascism to him – in the end really an expedient to win him over, but mainly to get him to intervene on his behalf so that Clelia Trotti's realm might open up to him a bit earlier than had been decreed – it sometimes happened that the shoemaker only listened, or replied coldly, in an exaggeratedly objective tone.

'No, I wouldn't say that,' he went as far as replying one evening, having given a peep outside to check. 'No, I wouldn't say that. Even the Fascists have done some good.'

He was clearly relishing a victory. Not only because Signorino Bruno, the son of those well-off folk in Via Madama whose shoes he'd resoled for almost twenty years, had come to pay him visits, but also because a moment ago he had enjoyed the luxury of conceding some small merit to a common enemy. He wasn't an upper-class gentleman, no, he seemed to be saying. He, Cesare Rovigatti, had been born and brought up among the poor, the persecuted, the oppressed. And so? Just because Cesare Rovigatti was only a shoemaker, did that now mean you could only expect from him obtuse rancour and blind, indiscriminate hatred? Ah no, that's too easy! Those times were over when the rich and powerful could make use of the working classes as cannon fodder, reserving a monopoly on fine sentiments for themselves! Enough of these misunderstandings! If someone had fooled themselves into thinking they could start these old tricks again now, entrusting the working classes with the noble task of doing their dangerous work for them, well then so much the worse for that someone.

He seemed to much prefer other topics to politics. Literature, for example.

Did Bruno like Victor Hugo?, he asked. What an unbeatable book, *Ninety-Three*! And *Les Misérables*? And *The Man Who Laughs*? And *Toilers of the Sea*? Although on a much lower level, only Francesco Domenico Guerrazzi in nineteenth-century Italy had managed to write a novel somewhat similar. And yet, all considered, what a disaster Italian literature was from the proletariat's point of view, taking into account the level of education available to him in our country! Among the poets, who was there to look to except Dante, 'the greatest poet in the world'? Those who came after had always written for the upper classes and not for the people. Petrarch, Ariosto, Tasso, Alfieri – oh yes, even Alfieri! – Foscolo: all of them fashioning stuff for the *élite*. As for *The Betrothed* – too much odour of incense, of the reactionary! No, if you wanted to read something worthy – modest, perhaps, but worthy – you had to leap forward to the Carducci of *The Love Song* or some of the social satires of Stecchetti. But on this subject, now, in the twentieth century, apart from 'that degenerate D'Annunzio', apart from Pascoli, how were things faring in the world of literature? He, unfortunately, hadn't the time to keep up. Closing at seven, the city library didn't allow any worker in the evening to profit from that public service. But Signorino Bruno didn't have the same constraints. Although, as a Jew, neither could *he* any longer frequent the city library, nevertheless he taught in the Jewish middle school in Via Vignatagliata and could consider himself a teacher. And so, educated as he was, and surely informed of all that's new, did he, Signorino Bruno, believe that in Italy, today, there were still any good writers?

Suddenly gripped by a deep sense of futility, almost of impotence, Bruno kept silent.

'In this field, I'd be willing to bet,' Rovigatti concluded, shaking his head, 'no one today's doing anything good or useful!'

But what Rovigatti was most at ease talking about was his own craft.

His was a humble craft, he said, one of the humblest, even: about this no one could be more convinced than he was. But thanks to it, not only had he been able to make ends meet since he was a boy, but also it meant he'd never had to bow down to anyone through all the years of the dictatorship. And then did Signorino Bruno think that being a shoemaker didn't provide him with interesting challenges? Any activity could provide those. You just need to exercise it with passion, succeed in winkling out its secrets.

He was speaking without the least bitterness at this point. And Bruno, listening to him, and bit by bit forgetting his own sadness, ended up feeling almost cheerful.

In his hands any misshapen and scuffed shoe always came alive. With infallible intuition, Rovigatti was able to reconstruct a character from the way a client had scuffed a toe, twisted an upper or worn down a heel.

'It'll be hard getting this person to pay up,' he would say, for example, handling some shoes of the tightest patent leather, which seemed new and yet hid considerable signs of wear under their pointed toes. The caution with which he proffered them for Bruno's inspection over the little workbench, for him to examine them with the interest they deserved, perfectly characterized their owner, who was Edelweiss Fegnagnani, no less, one of the most renowned 'decadents' of the city.

'And you, blonde beauty, be careful where you run off to!' he murmured with a sympathetic grin, passing his calloused thumb around the extraordinarily high heel, sharp as a dagger, of a little crocodile-skin shoe which a brisk, exuberant, triumphant style of walking had thoroughly consumed at the edges.

One evening he even showed Bruno, among others, the shoes of the honourable Bottecchiari, 'the prince of our forum', as he put it, not without sarcasm.

'He has some flaws, you can see,' he added a moment later, his eyes burning with combative enthusiasm, with tenacious loyalty, 'but he's someone in whom, thank God, one can still have some faith. What does it matter if he's become a bit bourgeois? He earns money, a great deal of it. He has a lovely house, a lovely wife . . . at least, lovely once, though fifty years will have taken a toll even on her . . . With his intelligence, his gifts as a speaker, even the Fascists respect him and court him. Last year they even wanted to give him a Party card. But d'you know what he said to them? He gave them a slap!'

Meanwhile his hands kept on turning over the honourable Bottecchiari's footwear, a pair of brown leather shoes with square toes – the shoes of a hearty optimist, weighing more than a hundred kilos, at whose side he had marched in the ranks of the Italian Socialist Party of Giacomo Matteotti, of Filippo Turati and Anna Kuliscioff, and together with him, in 1924, had been attacked in the downstairs salon of the Railworkers Food Co-operative, both of them escaping by sheer miracle through a back door.

He gestured with his chin in the direction of Via Fondo Banchetto.

Neither he nor the other friends from the old days, he continued, still met up with the honourable Bottecchiari, hadn't done so for almost twenty years, that was true. And yet, less than a week ago, seeing him passing the other way along the opposite pavement of the Giovecca (the other side of the barricade!, Bruno thought, suddenly swept up in a fellow feeling that bound him to Rovigatti, to Clelia Trotti, and to all the betrayed and forgotten poor of the city and of the country he imagined behind them, happy and grateful to be with them, now and for ever . . .), less than a week ago, Rovigatti was saying, the honourable Bottecchiari, jovial and easy-going as ever, had shouted out, waving an arm above his head: 'Ciao, Rovigatti!'

3.

One fine day the door of the house in Via Fondo Banchetto opened without the usual stout figure of Signora Codecà appearing at the threshold. It had to happen. In any decent fairy tale (it could have been three-thirty in the afternoon: there was indeed something unreal about the silence of that utterly deserted district), it's rare that things don't come to an end with the disappearance or transformation of the Monster. At a stroke the spell was broken: Signora Codecà had vanished into thin air. And, well, who but Clelia Trotti could that person be who had opened the door in her stead? It must surely be her, Bruno told himself. It could only be her, the withered, neglected little woman, a kind of nun, as people had described her! To convince himself, all he needed to do was look her in the eyes. They were still the striking eyes of the free, passionate girl who had modelled herself on Anna Kuliscioff, of the impetuous working-class heroine that the honourable Bottecchiari had loved in his youth . . .

Having shed her dragon skin, and resumed her true features, Clelia Trotti, now, like the princess in a fairy tale, smiled sweetly at the young man who stood on the cobblestones outside her door, at his air of surprise and perplexity. At this point a 'Come in – I know why you're here', would have been enough, and, as the little door closed behind them, shutting out the cottonwool-like hush of Via Fondo Banchetto, the fairy tale would have achieved its perfectly correct ending. But no, that welcome was not forthcoming. That sweet smile, somewhat disavowed by the clear expression in her sky-blue eyes, was merely questioning. It seemed to say 'Who are you? And what do you want?' So much so that, at least this time, Bruno had little difficulty in understanding. It was clear, he thought. His name up till now had never been mentioned to Clelia Trotti, neither by Signora Codecà nor even by Rovigatti. It was necessary, then, across the threshold still denied to him, to declare his name and surname: 'Bruno' and 'Lattes', syllable by syllable. This, in any case, was enough for the puzzlement that covered Trotti's face – sincere puzzlement and a trusting abandon, while her pale eyes seemed washed in a wave of generous compassion – to give way to a clearer, more realistic perspective on the situation.

'Take care as *she* is under surveillance!' the honourable Bottecchiari had said, lowering his voice to a whisper. He was referring to the police, the *Organizzazione per la Vigilanza e la Repressione dell'Antifascismo*.[13] But yet again things, when considered more closely, turned out to be different from what they seemed.

'Let's go and talk in the dining-room,' murmured the old schoolteacher once she had ushered Bruno into the hallway and shut the door.

She preceded him on tiptoe down a dark, narrow, damp corridor. Following her in the same manner, trying not to make any noise and at the same time watching her move with all the stealth she could muster, he found it easy to guess why. Clelia Trotti was under surveillance mainly *at home*. Signora Codecà and her husband (the former a full-time elementary-school teacher, the latter cashier for the Agricola Bank, the stronghold of the city's landowning middle class) were Clelia Trotti's true jailors. And *OVRA*? *OVRA* knew perfectly well what it was doing. Assigning the 'cautioned' sixty-year-old to the domestic control of this worthy couple, persons clearly possessing too much good sense to put up with their unwelcome guest of a

---

13 See the footnote about this organization on p. 80.

relative receiving suspect visitors, the organization merely needed to appear every now and then. In the meantime, it could, very tranquilly, doze off.

They entered the small, ground-floor dining-room. Bruno looked around. So it was here, he said to himself, that Clelia Trotti spent the most part of her days, talking herself hoarse giving lessons to the infants and children of the neighbourhood! So this was her prison!

The furniture in pale wood was cheap, but not without ridiculous pretensions. The faded green woollen cloth, stained with ink, which covered the table in the centre, the Murano-style glass chandelier suspended from the ceiling, the accountant's diploma inscribed to the head of the house, Evaristo Codecà, in ruled lines and in florid gothic script, that hung in its glory among wretched pictures of seascapes and mountain landscapes, the huge dark shape of a grandfather clock in the corner, with a dry, resonant, menacing tick-tock, even the ray of sunlight which – from the solitary window, the custodian of a little huddle of pot plants – penetrated the room, revealing on the opposite side in the centre of a small, bare wickerwork sofa, a horse's head painted in oils on the hempen cover of a fat cushion; and there, at last, on the other side of the table, smiling, it's true, but with an apologetic look, as if asking for a bit of indulgence, sat the old revolutionary who had seen Anna Kuliscioff and Andrea Costa with her own eyes, who had argued about Socialism with Filippo Turati, who played a by-no-means-secondary part in the famous Red Week of the Romagna in 1914, now reduced to speaking in muffled tones, raising her eyes now and then to the ceiling to signal that her sister or brother-in-law might at any moment come down from upstairs to surprise and interrupt them. Or else she remained silent, with her open hand half-raised and the forefinger of her other hand at her lips (the pendulum clock chimed hoarsely during one of these silences, and at the same time a low clucking of hens could be heard from the garden), like a schoolgirl scared of being caught out . . . In that place like the depths of a well, in that sort of vulnerable den, everything spoke to Bruno of boredom, of accidie, of long years of stingy, inglorious segregation and oblivion. He couldn't, at a certain point, avoid asking himself, Was it then really worth the trouble to struggle through life in a way so different from how, for example, the honourable Bottecchiari had behaved, if time, which weakens and overturns everything, had extended its fell, corrupting hand on all alike? Clelia Trotti had never bowed her neck, had always preserved her soul in all its purity. On the contrary, the honourable Bottecchiari, although he never accepted the Fascist Party card, had fully involved himself in society in his maturer years. Without anyone complaining about or being scandalized by it, he had blithely become part of the administrative council of the Agricola Bank. So, considering the outcome, which of the two had made the right choices in life? And what had he come for, enrolling himself so late in the day, if not precisely for that: to realize that the better world, the just and decent society of which Clelia Trotti represented the living proof and the relic, would never return? He watched her, the pathetic, persecuted anti-Fascist, the pitiful prisoner, and was unable to detach his eyes from the dark furrow, clearly visible, which, just under her white hair gathered in a bun at her nape, ran all around her thin wrinkled neck. What kind of help, he thought, continuing to stare at that poor, ill-washed neck, could he expect from Clelia Trotti, from Rovigatti, and from that humble circle of their friends of whose existence no one could even be sure? For goodness' sake! To extract himself from that grotesque conversation he would have to get up and go from there as soon as possible, and perhaps from that point on to listen a bit more attentively to what his father never tired of advising him. That might be a good idea. Why not just for once pay attention to what his father said? From September last year, his father had lost no opportunity to tell him to take himself off to *Eretz*, as he was in the habit of saying, or to the United States, or South America. He was still young, his father would insistently say, his whole life was before him. He should emigrate, put down roots abroad. There was still a chance. Before the following summer Italy would certainly not yet have entered the war. And carrying the passport of a persecuted Jew, no one would have the will to refuse him entry . . .

'Be patient, I beg you,' Clelia Trotti whispered in the meantime, 'but in this house I'm merely a guest. My sister and brother-in-law –' she added, her blue eyes staring into Bruno's, showing once more the joy of confiding, the certainty of not being mistaken in having trusted him – 'my sister and brother-in-law, since I returned from internal exile, and so for quite a few years, have taken me in, and have no other thought –' here she shook her head and laughed – 'but to stop me committing any further folly.'

She twisted her lips.

'They keep me under surveillance –' her gaze suddenly serious, almost severe – 'and poke their noses into everything I do, believe me it's worse than being a baby. I understand. For people who don't think as *we* do . . . who have a political viewpoint utterly different from *ours* . . . good people, you know, two hearts of gold . . . I understand that behaving the way they unfortunately do towards me might seem the right thing to do. They claim they do it for my own good. Perhaps so. But how annoying it is!'

'Is your sister the one who always comes to open the door?'

'Yes, it's my sister, but why?' replied the schoolmistress in alarm. 'Does that mean . . . ? Oh, you poor thing!' she exclaimed, joining her small bony hands together, her right hand's index and middle fingers stained with nicotine. 'Who knows how many times Giovanna will have forced you to make the trip to no avail!'

'One day she'd say one thing, the next another. They were excuses, I could easily see. But I could only suppose you were aware of that. And now . . .'

'Oh, you poor thing!' repeated Clelia Trotti. 'And there I was talking about what was right! No. Within certain limits I can understand it, but this is going much too far. They will hear from me.'

She remained silent for some seconds, as though meditating on the seriousness of the judgement that had been imposed on her and the measures she would have to take to assert her rights. And yet, at the same time, you could see she was thinking of something else. Something that, despite herself, gave her some pleasure.

'Listen. How did you come by my address? It can't have been that easy for you to procure it, I imagine.'

Within the Walls

'A couple of months ago, I had the idea of going to ask for it from the lawyer Bottecchiari,' Bruno replied, looking elsewhere.

And since Signora Trotti didn't inquire any further, he added: 'Bottecchiari is an old friend of the family. I was counting on him knowing where to direct me. But he didn't know, or didn't want to tell me, anything very clear. He advised me to call in on Cesare Rovigatti, you know, the shoemaker who has his workshop near here in Piazza Santa Maria in Vado. Luckily I knew him very well, and . . .'

'Our little Cesare, yes, indeed. Very dear to us. But I don't understand how . . . He himself could easily have spoken to me about you! Don't you see? For one reason or another there's no one who doesn't feel compelled to act in the oddest way towards me. And they don't understand that, with this system, gradually making everything a desert around me, it's as if they're taking away the air I breathe. Better to be in prison, then!'

There was fatigue, disgust and deep bitterness in the tone with which she pronounced these words. Bruno looked her in the face. But her intensely blue eyes, steady and dry under her grey, knitted eyebrows, were full of hope, as though she doubted everything and everybody except him.

Suddenly the door opened. Someone looked in. It was Signora Codecà.

'Who's there?' had asked the familiar, hateful voice before the salt-and-pepper head-of-hair poked in to investigate.

The diffident gaze of Signora Codecà fell on Bruno.

'Ah,' she said coldly, 'I didn't know you had a visitor.'

'But it's a friend! It's Signor Lattes . . .' Clelia Trotti hurried to explain, agitated. 'Bruno Lattes!'

'Pleasure to meet you!' said Signora Codecà, without taking a step forward. 'At last you've found her, eh?' she added in a sour tone in Bruno's direction without actually looking at him.

She drew back a little.

From the dark of the corridor a little eight- or nine-year-old child came forward with a frightened look. Three white horizontal lines were drawn across the front of his black smock.

'Go on in,' Signora Codecà encouraged him.

Giorgio Bassani

And then, turning to her sister: 'Don't worry, I'll accompany Signor Lattes out.'

When they had once again assumed their familiar positions, with her massive person blocking the door and Bruno looking up at her from the cobbled street, Signora Codecà spoke again.

'I'm not sure if my sister remembered to tell you, but after tomorrow at the latest, Clelia will really have to go away. On a trip, a rather long one. How long? I don't know for sure, perhaps several weeks . . . perhaps several months . . . so for the moment it's useless for you to pay any more visits. Try to understand. You'd be doing us a favour, Signor Lattes, if you'd be considerate about this. *I'm saying this also for your own sake . . .*'

She stressed these last words with a plaintive, pleading look. Then, as she drew back and slowly shut the door in Bruno's face, she added in a whisper: 'We're under surveillance, d'you understand?'

That very night, returning home as usual, very late, and without even having phoned around eight o'clock to tell them not to expect him for supper – he'd spent the evening first at the cinema and then seated by the billiards table in a bar outside Porta Reno – Bruno was taken by surprise in the street by the snow.

To start with it was a sifting of tiny flakes milling lightly around the streetlamps. But shortly after, in Via Madama, as he tried to fit his key into the front door, the flakes had already become so thick and heavy that in no time his face was drenched.

He kept on fumbling with the key, and in doing so, as the castle clock had begun to toll the hours, he tried to count them. One, two, three, four. Four o'clock: very late indeed, but for all that he had little hope his father would have given up waiting and switched off the light – he would only turn it off after he heard him groping past his bedroom door on tiptoe, and his father would let him understand, by coughing and grumbling, that he had stayed awake and worried till that late hour. On the other hand, all the better. Perhaps this night he could be exempted from the tired, stupid saga of tiptoeing along the dark corridor. If his father was still not asleep, fine. He would turn the main light on and resolutely enter his bedroom. He already knew what his father would speak to him about.

Within the Walls

And yet, when he found himself in the large entrance hall, at the end of which, across the dividing wall, he could see the dark garden plants, he became aware of a faint light filtering round the door of the ground-floor room that served him as a study. He drew close. Slowly, he opened the door. His father was there, seated in the armchair next to the table. Wrapped in a woollen blanket, he slept with his head inclined against his shoulder.

He stepped noiselessly into the room, and leant against the wall beside the door.

He'd never come home, he reflected, as late as this. That was perhaps why at a certain point his father had decided to get up from bed and go downstairs, like this, in his nightshirt and slippers. Who could say? It might have been that he'd thought to take the opportunity of a thorough discussion with him about emigrating to Palestine or America, a topic which every time his father had broached it, he'd responded to coldly or even rudely. If he waited for him down in the study, his father had perhaps told himself, the two of them would be able to talk, or even quarrel, for as long as they wanted. Their voices wouldn't have woken anyone.

He moved on tiptoe, grimacing. And he was about to touch the sleeper's left hand, resting as though dead over the *Il Resto di Carlino*,[14] the newspaper open and unfolded over his knees – his right hand, on which his forehead was resting, was instinctively placed to shield his half-closed eyelids from the light of the table lamp – when a sudden pang of sorrow interrupted his gesture midway.

He retracted his arm and took a step backwards.

But instead of turning and leaving, he halted to look at his father's scrawny, frail temples, more cartilage than bone, and his white, feathery, weightless hair, in its lightness and whiteness so similar to Clelia Trotti's. How many more years would his father live? And Clelia Trotti? Would the two of them live long enough to witness the conclusion of the tragedy that was convulsing the world?

Although finished and near to death, both of them in the end were

---

[14] A Bologna newspaper which was founded in 1885, and was under Fascist control from 1923 to 1943.

still dreaming their dreams. From her prison in Via Fondo Banchetto, Clelia Trotti was dreaming that the rebirth of Italian socialism would occur thanks to the infusion of youthful blood into the Party's old, decrepit veins. From the Ghetto of Via Madama, where with morose delectation he had holed up – the beloved, irreplaceable Merchants' Club had naturally expelled him, so now he stayed at home reading the newspapers and listening to Radio London – the lawyer Lattes dreamt of the 'brilliant career' which was bound to await his little son in America or in *Eretz*. But he, Bruno, the little son, what would he do? Stay or go? His papa was mistaken about the power of discrimination: the police headquarters would never issue him with a passport. And since the war, now only just begun, would last who knows how long, since the trap now sprung had rendered any escape impossible, since the only road now was obviously the one that would lead everyone, without exclusion, towards a future without hope, it was better to join in voluntarily, if only for compassion and humility, in the desperate hobbies, the wretched, miserable delusions of onanistic prisoners that were shared by his fellow travellers.

Still on tiptoe, he went towards the window.

After having half-closed one of the two shutters, he looked out through the steamed-up panes between the slats. The snow continued to fall. After some hours it would be piled high, would have extended its oppressive hush over the whole city, a prison and a ghetto for everyone.

4.

In the end, Signora Codecà had her way. She asked that her house should not become a den of conspirators. And, finally, she had revealed herself, had thrown her hand down on the table, all the cards of an undoubtedly zealous jailor, and yet not treacherous, only fearful.

Whatever she said or thought, in all probability OVRA had completely forgotten about 36, Via Fondo Banchetto. For a long time, no policeman had shown up at dusk to check whether the

Within the Walls

'cautioned' Trotti, Clelia, was to be found at her prescribed and proper domicile. Yet it was better not to contradict Signora Codecà. Better to let her play the role of a strict and incorruptible spy which she herself had assumed. Never to lose sight of her subversive sister, who, after her spell of internal exile, had been sentenced to ten supplementary years of enforced residence with a daily obligation to be indoors by dusk and to report every week at the police station to sign in the special register of the 'cautioned'; to rush to the door at every loud ring, without ever forgetting to wear the Fascist badge in full view on top of the black smock of a teacher in regular employment – even Signora Codecà had the right to a small raft of illusions, an element of play, necessary to anyone who wants to survive! And Clelia Trotti? Did she truly want to be visited? To leave the house with a furtive air, peep out through the upstairs shutters, to rapidly turn the corner into Via Coperta – if there was something that gave her pleasure, surely it must be this? Sooner or later it would be she herself who would make an appearance.

One morning, about two months later, while he was teaching in a classroom of the Jewish School in Via Vignatagliata, Bruno saw the janitoress' head peeping gingerly round the door.

'May I?'

'What is it?'

'There's a lady outside who wants to see you.'

Scuffing her slippers on the brickwork floor and prompting the usual hum of mirth, the janitoress came towards the teacher's desk.

'What should I tell her?' she asked worriedly.

Of an indeterminable age, short, round, with two oily, shining strips of raven hair which descended from the top of her head to frame a sleepy-looking, sheepish face, she was one of the least ancient of those recruited from the hospice for the old in Via Vittoria by the engineer Cohen when, in October 1938, it was necessary to find space on the second floor of the kindergarten for the older children expelled from the state middle schools.

'Tell her to wait for the bell to go off,' Bruno replied, so irritably that the pupils suddenly went quiet. 'How many times must I tell you not to disturb me during lessons?'

Giorgio Bassani

It was Clelia Trotti, it had to be her.

Continuing to explain things to the pupils and to ask them questions, in his mind's eye he saw her waiting in the adjoining vestibule. She was reading the big tablets full of the names of benefactors affixed to the walls between the washed-out doors of the classrooms; she was contemplating, one by one, the varnished clay busts of Victor Emmanuel II, of Umberto I and of Victor Emmanuel III, placed in the niches of the wall around the Victory Dispatch.[15] Every now and then she went to look out of the two big windows opposite, both of them thrown open wide . . .

At last, the bell rang. Pouring out of the classrooms into the hallway, the children rushed headlong down the big central staircase. When Bruno, too, had gone out into the now deserted hallway, spotting the little woman in hat and grey suit down there, standing still, with her back to him looking at Diaz's proclamation, for some moments he was disconcerted. He was hoping that, hearing his steps, she would turn round with a start, and smile at him with that kind smile of hers, as though close to tears, to look him in the face with her blue eyes flashing the same ironic, sad and generous expression they had when he had first told her his name. Only then would he truly recognize her.

'It's been many years since I read the Dispatch of the 4th of November 1918!' said Clelia Trotti, even before she shook his hand, signalling with her chin towards the tablet. 'I needed to come all the way here to do that!'

They faced each other by the big window that overlooked the inner courtyard garden, with its stricken little trees in the spring sunlight crowded with chirping sparrows, and they rested their elbows on the iron rail.

'What a lovely time of the year, isn't it?' the schoolmistress said, looking out towards the red vista of roofs that opened before them, beyond the garden walls.

'It is indeed.'

---

15 The *Bollettino della Vittoria* is the final address to the army and the nation issued by the chief of staff, General Armando Diaz, at the conclusion of the Battle of Vittorio Veneto, which ended the First World War in Italy.

He observed her from the corner of his eye. She had taken care to spruce herself up, and applied powder as far down as her neck.

'You feel yourself coming alive again,' she continued, half-closing her eyes against the glare.

And then, after a pause, but still with a sense of inner joy: 'How right we were though, we Socialists – to tell the truth, it wasn't just a few of us, at that stage, who thought otherwise – to hear our death knell in the bells rung for the Italian victory of 1918! "The valleys, they had invaded, with confidence and pride . . ." Already concealed within those words is the Fascist movement, the arrogant rhetoric of these last twenty years.'

Suddenly, emerging out of the stagnant depths of his own bitterness, Bruno felt a violent impulse to hurt her, to do harm to her.

'Why d'you want to fool yourself?' he interrupted. 'Why maintain the deception? As you know, in Ferrara all of us Jews, or nearly all of us, were nothing other than bourgeoisie – I say *were*, since now, perhaps all for the better, we no longer belong to any class, we make up a social group apart, as in medieval times. We were nearly all of us retail traders or wholesale merchants, professionals of various stripes, landowners, and therefore, as you have taught me, nearly all Fascists. Of necessity. You have no idea how many of us even today have remained fervent patriots!'

'You mean nationalists?' Clelia Trotti gently corrected him.

'Call them what you like. My father, for example, went to fight on the Carso as a volunteer. In 1919, returning from the front, he chanced on a march of workers, who, seeing him in officer's uniform, literally covered him with spit. Today, obviously, he isn't a Fascist any longer, despite the fact that it was actually his Fascist Party card of 1922 that earned us some exemptions. Now he only thinks about the Palestinian fatherland. And yet, I wouldn't swear that General Diaz's sentences, which continue to make such an impression on the imaginations of most of my – what should I call them? – my co-religionists, will have entirely stopped having an impact on the imagination of those who share yours!'

'What you say seems to me very understandable,' Clelia Trotti calmly replied. 'You explain it very well.'

She didn't seem in the least disappointed, but perhaps, once again, somewhat saddened.

She sighed.

'The First World War has been a great disaster,' she said. 'How many mistakes even *we* made! Nonetheless, you seem to me too pessimistic. Fair enough: in general terms, you're right. Why not take yourself into account, though? You're different, you're not like the others, and your example is more than enough to show that every rule has its exception. And you're young, you have your whole life before you. For the young like you who have grown up under Fascism, there is a great deal for you to do!'

Hearing Clelia Trotti using the very same phrases as his father, Bruno raised his head. He had again turned to look out of the window. The future she saw was down there, where the last houses in Ferrara, their roofs a dark rusty colour, gave way in the direction of the sea to the blue-green of the endless countryside.

A few months later Fascist Italy also decided to enter the lists.

'At last!' Clelia Trotti exclaimed, joyful and breathless, that very evening of 10 June, as she entered the study in Via Madama.

'At last!' she repeated, as she dropped into the armchair.

She leant her neck back on the green velvet headrest and closed her eyes. It wasn't the first time that, making the most of the darkness and defying all prohibitions, she had come to visit Bruno. And yet the intensity of excitement which these clandestine visits gave her from the first showed no signs of diminishing.

When her breathing had returned to normal, she immediately said that Fascism, with that mad gesture of declaring war, had signed its own death warrant. She was sure of it, she affirmed, and began to explain with extraordinary heat and passion why she was so sure of her prediction.

Bruno stared at her in silence.

Her good faith was unquestionable, he thought, no one had the right to doubt it. And yet why not admit it? Wasn't the look that shone in her eyes, above all, the certainty – now that leaving Italy had become truly impossible – that he would no longer be able to dodge the task that she had assigned him in her heart of hearts, nor slip out of her hands, as up until yesterday she had feared he might? Undoubtedly there was something of that. Even though, from the expression her mouth had already taken on, tender but at the same time sceptical, it was more than evident that she first of all – she who might be his mother! – would forbid any comparison to be made between the boy before her and Mauro Bottecchiari, the companion of her youth, whom Italy's entry into the war in long-ago 1915 had offered the political pretext of his being rid of her.

In the early stages, their meetings in his downstairs study were on a fairly frequent basis. Everything was done lightly, of course, as a game, the kind of game prisoners might play, steeped in bitterness and in the absence of everyday consolations, and Bruno took some pleasure from it, even from that air of erotic subterfuge which inevitably hovered over their meetings – always occurring after supper; every now and then she would be late, and he would be reading a book or preparing a lesson while he waited – and especially for her light, complicit knock on the blinds outside, which would startle him.

As soon as she came in, Clelia Trotti would sit herself down in the armchair. But sometimes, without even taking off her grey cotton gloves – despite the heat that soaked her forehead with sweat, she would never take off her hat – she would at once get up again and go towards one of the four glass-fronted bookcases symmetrically disposed along the lower part of the study's walls, and remain there with her nose against the glass. Her unwillingness to open the bookcase doors showed a kind of tact. She confined herself to peering through the glass and reading the titles of the books with the help of an eyeglass she would draw from her big black leather bag.

'Why not take some away with you?' Bruno, from behind a table heaped with papers, would encourage her. 'I'd gladly loan you any of them.'

She shook her head. With all the lessons she had to give, she wouldn't have time to read them.

'Besides, I'm so behind the times in all cultural matters,' she confided to him one evening, 'that to get up to date would require an effort beyond me. For example, I've always wanted to read a book by

Benedetto Croce; I'm not sure, maybe one of his less abstruse works, one of his historical studies. Year after year, I've put off doing so, a little because I imagine the fear it would cause my sister Giovanna, poor thing, should she find that sort of stuff in the house, and also a little because of reservations ... to do with socialism. Decades have passed, and here we are, and it no longer seems worth the trouble. When I was a girl, I had a passion for philosophy. In those days it was all Comte, Spencer, Ardigò and Haeckel with his Monism.'

She smiled.

Then, with a tinge of shyness in her eyes: 'You, though, are bound to know the works of Croce well, isn't that so?'

It was a reference to what Bruno himself, though he immediately regretted it, had once been unable to stop himself from saying: that he wasn't a Socialist and in all probability never would be.

Yet stronger than any grief, any regret that she was not at a level to be able to teach him anything, she was undoubtedly consoled by the belief that this itself was as it should be: that he wasn't a Socialist, yes, but something other, something new. Socialists of the old school would not know how to confront the future, the years that were awaiting Italy and the world beyond the war that had just begun, years which would only be reached after having paid who knows what reckoning of blood and tears. 'We lot are over the hill, a bunch of dinosaurs,' she used to say. It was as though she were attesting that tomorrow, in their stead, there would be a need for the young like him, Bruno, who would be Socialists without being such. Only thus would it be possible, when the moment arrived, for the Communists to be given a hard time, even though they were 'giants', though they too, especially in their 'methods', now belonged in the past.

Towards the end of September, *OVRA* unexpectedly reappeared on the scene.

One day, towards dusk, an agent of the political wing in plain clothes came to ask if Signora Trotti was 'at her domicile'. Winded, Signora Codecà replied that she was at home. But the woman's agitated state must have made the official suspicious, and he wouldn't go away without having assured himself with his own eyes, albeit with a profusion of apologies, that everything was in order. One could no longer be sure. Fearing that this sudden awakening of the police signalled a harsher policy of control towards the 'cautioned', Clelia Trotti decided to renounce her nocturnal escapades for some time after. Bruno and she had to see each other in the daytime, as it were by chance, avoiding, naturally, any further visits to the study in Via Madama.

So every now and then, even if not with the same frequency as before, and arranging their appointments by way of Rovigatti – who, being jealously possessive of Trotti, was ill-disposed to help – they began to meet in the Piazza della Certosa. From his perspective, Rovigatti wasn't mistaken, Bruno could see that. What had they to say to each other or to do together, he and Clelia Trotti, that was worth the risk? It wasn't as though the two of them saw each other, as Rovigatti insinuated, just to talk about Radio London or Colonel Stevens. Certainly not for that. But in the present, tense situation, was it really worth provoking the police?

He tried to pass on the shoemaker's comments to the schoolmistress, attempting also to offer bland justifications for them. In vain. Every time he returned to the topic, she shrugged her shoulders with annoyance.

'What a bore he is!' she sighed.

'Poor little Cesare!' she laughed one evening, and never before had she seemed so youthful. 'He acts like that because he's very fond of me. D'you know when it was we first got to know each other?'

'Before the First World War, I imagine.'

'Oh, much earlier than that! From back in elementary school. We both lived in Vicolo del Gregorio.'

'So you came to know Bottecchiari much later.'

'Much later,' she replied drily.

And she gave him a look with a hint of irony, and seemed more youthful than ever.

In the bright late afternoons of September the huge field in front of the church of San Cristoforo was crowded, as it always was when the weather was fine, with children, nursemaids and young couples.

Bruno Lattes and Clelia Trotti would speak, sitting close to each other at the edge of the churchyard for the most part, but sometimes on the grass, in the margin of shadow that grew slowly at the southern limit of the portico with the descent of the sun, on the side of Via Borso.

'It's lovely here, don't you think?' said Trotti, her eyes turned towards the square. 'It doesn't at all seem as if we're in a graveyard.'

'I've never understood,' she said on one occasion, 'why the dead are kept segregated from us, as is our custom, so that if you want to visit them you have to get permission, as you would for a prison visit. Napoleon was undoubtedly a great man as he imposed on Europe, as well as on Italy, via our Cisalpine Republic, the democratic and social triumphs of the Revolution. But as far as his famous edict on cemeteries goes, I remain of the same opinion as the poet of *The Sepulchres*.[16] D'you believe me? I'd like them to bury me right here outside, in this lovely field, with all this noise of life going on around, even if that would cost me eternal excommunication.'

She started laughing.

'It's only a dream, I know,' she quickly added, 'a pious desire that won't ever come true. Apart from some years in prison, some others in internal exile and now this invigilated freedom, what have I done in my life that's so important to deserve a tomb among the illustrious figures of our city, even the heretical ones? To be sure, I haven't even been beaten up. The Fascists were more refined with me. When I was leaving the Umberto I elementary school in Via Bersaglieri del Po in 1922, they confined themselves to making me drink a half ounce of cod-liver oil and covering my face with soot. And so what! If it hadn't been for the children who were standing there watching, and many of them crying from fear, it wouldn't have upset me that much, I can assure you. There was hardly the call to come in a group of twenty or thirty, with cudgels, daggers, skulls on their berets, to subdue a woman on her own. A nice show of force! While I was swallowing my portion of cod-liver oil, I knew

---

16 Ugo Foscolo (1778–1827), an important Italian poet whose most famous work is *Dei sepolcri*.

that the Blackshirts would have achieved nothing by it except to heap general disapproval on themselves.'

But what she always preferred to talk about was her past as a prisoner and internal exile.

'Prison gives you a real schooling,' she said on another evening, lighting a Macedonia cigarette with the lit stub of the last (a vice, she explained, that – to illustrate the point – she'd picked up in prison), 'at least that's so if it doesn't go on too long and that it doesn't break the will or weaken the moral fibre. As regards my own experience, I'm grateful to fate that I wasn't spared the test. Solitude, concentration, having no company but our own . . . these are worth learning. And to know oneself, to struggle with one's own tendencies and to emerge from that sometimes victorious, can only happen within the four walls of a cell. When I got out of prison in 1930, I left my number 36 (d'you see the coincidence? – the same number as my sister's house) with real sadness, as if I were leaving behind a part of myself. Each wall, each corner, every tiny thing carried a trace of suffering. The truth is that the places where you have wept, where you've suffered, where you've had to find the many inner resources to keep hoping and resisting, are the ones you grow fondest of. Take yourself, for example. You could have left, like so many of your co-religionists, and after what you've had to put up with, you'd have had every right. But you made a different choice. You preferred to stay here, to struggle and suffer. And now this country, this city where you were born, where you grew up and became a man, has become doubly yours. You will never, ever abandon it.'

She would always end like this. Having started, as usual, by telling a story about herself and her own life, she would soon steer the talk towards Bruno and what she thought he should be doing in the immediate future.

On his behalf for quite some time she had been preparing useful contacts with the city's principal anti-Fascists, she would say, and so, for this very reason, she'd already entrusted Rovigatti with the task of preparing the ground for his imminent visits.

The first people he should approach were undoubtedly the Socialists. But he should take care. Not the notary Licci, a distinctly sour and cantankerous 'maximalist' – better leave him to stew in his own juices until he himself decided to shake off his grumpiness and seek out his old friends. Bruno needed to see first of all the lawyers, Baruffaldi, Polenghi and Tamagnini, all three of them Reformists eager to act, and after, returning to the topic of Bottecchiari, to try to link up with his nephew Nino, who for some six or seven months had been taken on as an assistant in his uncle's office. He was without doubt a very bright and able young man, considering that he'd been able to make an impression even on the *Gruppi Universitari Fascisti*, where he'd been assigned very important roles in the last two years. She urged Bruno to get in contact with him soon, to avert the possibility that one day or another he'd be lured by some new 'totalitarian siren'.

But then, after the Socialists, he needed to get to know the *Repubblicani-storici*, such as the dentist Canella, the tailor Squarcia, the chemist Riccoboni. These, too, had of late shown unambiguous signs of wanting to shift, of being ready, because of the shared aims of the struggle, to forget their everlasting rancour and anti-Socialist prejudices.

As for the Catholics, their circle, in this respect similar to the Communist one, remained something of a self-contained world which would be hard to enter. All the same, the lawyer Galassi-Tarabini, he at least, was a remarkably open-minded type. Already in close contact with both Count Gròsoli and Don Sturzo, opposed by the Fascist clerics since Pius XI exalted Mussolini to the point of calling him the Man of Providence – yes, he was a person of real integrity, not to be overlooked in any way. And the same could be said of the engineer Sears, a liberal, leaning to the right, but still good-hearted, and of Dr Herzen, a committed Zionist, agreed, but perhaps recruitable to the cause of Italian anti-Fascism, especially if he were to be approached by a fellow Jew.

And finally he ought to meet up with Alfio Mori, the friend and in some ways the disciple of Antonio Gramsci – they'd got to know each other in prison – the person from whom it's said that his comrade Ercoli, every time he secretly re-enters the country from the Soviet Union, most willingly accepts advice. Mori was the most important of them all, and, as such, was most keenly under surveillance. He would always need to move with extreme prudence. For example, he might arrange a meeting, and Mori wouldn't turn up. A second one, and Mori would be absent once again. Only on the fifth or the sixth appointment might he finally decide to appear. So it was indispensable to be armed with patience. And if he, Bruno, was prepared to be patient, he might indeed manage also to have a talk with Mori . . .

She talked on and on. The shadows of the steles and gravestones slowly lengthened on the grass, the field little by little shed its crowd of visitors, and some enamoured couples moved off in the direction of the bastions.

That evening Bruno was stretched out, as was his habit, at the feet of Clelia Trotti. As he listened without much attention to what the teacher was saying, he noticed a tall, slim, blond boy leaning on the handlebars of his bicycle some twenty metres away.

His head immersed in the pink sheets of the sports pages, he looked as though he were waiting for someone. And there on cue, at the far end of the square, almost running to reach him, was a girl, she, too, blonde and very beautiful, who, while continuing to cross the open field, turned every three or four steps to look back towards Via Borso as if she feared she were being pursued.

But of course it wasn't true. She was merely acting.

Once she had reached her friend, she was the first, like a good actress, to slip down on to the grass, with the rapid, graceful movements of one hand arranging her pleated, white woollen dress around her legs. With the other hand she tugged affectionately at the boy, who had remained standing, to sit down beside her.

Soon the two of them were sitting close to each other, beside the bicycle with their backs turned. Their young heads were so close as to be touching. Suffused with the mild air, delighted by the light touching of their bodies, it seemed as though they had no need to speak. 'Who are they? What are their names?' Bruno was wondering while the voice of Clelia Trotti sounded distantly in his ear, an incomprehensible hum. He couldn't remember their names. He was quite sure, though, that they were both still at school, perhaps at the *liceo classico*, and that they both belonged to one of the city's upper-middle-class families.

Ten or so minutes passed.

Suddenly Bruno saw the boy move. He got back to his feet, calmly picked up the bicycle and then grasped his friend by her wrist. Letting herself go heavy, she now laughed with a lazy flirtatiousness, leaning her whole neck back.

They began to move off in the direction of the walls, crossing the field on a diagonal.

'Why don't we go down there too?' Bruno asked.

Stretching out his left arm, he pointed at the Mura degli Angeli still in full sunlight.

'But it's late. I'm afraid we won't have time,' Clelia Trotti, interrupted mid-sentence, replied. 'You know I have to turn in along with the hens!'

'What will it matter just this once? We'll be able to see a magnificent sunset.'

He had already stood up. He stretched out a hand to help her get up, and then they walked on.

The young couple were about fifty metres ahead of them. The boy was sitting on his bike, and every now and then, to keep his balance, he encircled his companion's shoulders with his right arm. Bruno watched them with an insatiable interest. 'Who are they? What are their names?' he kept muttering under his breath. They seemed to him more than beautiful – marvellous, incomparable. There they were: the champions, the prototypes of their race! he said to himself with hatred and a desperate love, half-closing his eyes. Their blood was better than his, their souls were finer than his. If he wasn't mistaken, the girl's hair was tied at the back with a red ribbon. The little light that remained seemed to concentrate itself on that ribbon.

Oh, to be them, to be one of them, despite everything!

'I did well to let you persuade me. From the top of the wall we'll be able to enjoy a truly extraordinary sunset,' Clelia Trotti calmly observed.

Bruno turned round. So she had seen nothing. Yet again she'd noticed nothing at all. And now once more she'd continued with what she'd been saying. Talking as if to herself. As if pursuing her dream. Lost, as ever, in the unending, lonely ravings of a convict.

He shivered.

Perhaps one day she would understand who Bruno Lattes was, he thought, turning back to look before him. But that day, if it should ever arrive, was still surely a long way off.

A Night of '43

I.

At first you might not be aware of it. But once you've been seated for a few minutes at one of the small outside tables of the Caffè della Borsa, with the sheer crag of the Clocktower before you and, a bit to the right, the crenellated terrace of the Orangery, the whole thing dawns on you. This is what happens. In summer as in winter, in rain or shine, it's very unusual for whoever crosses that stretch of Corso Roma to prefer keeping to the pavement opposite that runs along the dark-brown back of the Castle moat. If anyone does so, then it's sure to be a tourist, finger wedged between the pages of the *Touring Guide* and gaze tilted upwards, or a travelling salesman who, with leather bag under his arm, is hurrying towards the station, or a farm worker from the Po delta come to the city for the market who, waiting to take the local afternoon bus back to Comacchio or Codigoro, with evident embarrassment lugs his body weighed down with the food and wine he consumed a little after midday in a dive in San Romano. In short, it could be anyone, except someone from Ferrara.

The visitor goes past, and the caffè regulars stare and grin. Yet, at certain hours of the day, those eyes stare in a strange way, even the breath is cut short. The boredom and laziness of the provinces might be the seed for all kinds of imaginary massacres. It's as though the pavement stones opposite were to be blown to bits by the explosion of a mine detonated by the unwary visitor's foot. Or else as though a rapid burst of bullets from the Fascist machine-gunner who, as it happened, fired precisely from here, from under the portico of the Caffè della Borsa one night in December 1943, murdering eleven citizens on that stretch of pavement, should

Within the Walls

make the incautious passer-by perform the same brief, ghastly jig, all startled twists and jumps, that in the moment of death the victims undoubtedly performed before falling lifeless one on top of the other – those whom History has for years consecrated as the very first victims of the Italian civil war.

Of course, none of this happens. No mine explodes, no machine-gun returns to pepper with bullet holes the low wall opposite. And so this visitor who, let's suppose, has come to Ferrara to admire its fine artistic heritage, can pass by in front of the little marble plaques bearing the engraved names of the executed persons without their thoughts being assailed by the least disturbance.

And yet, sometimes, something does happen.

One suddenly hears a voice. It isn't a powerful voice, but rather a raw, cracked voice as boys at the onset of puberty have. And as it emerges from the puny chest of Pino Barilari, the owner of the adjoining pharmacy, who, at one of the windows of the apartment above, remains invisible to whoever is seated below, to them it really sounds like it has descended from the heavens. The voice says 'Beware, young man!' or 'Careful!' or 'Whoa there!' It's not, I repeat, as though these words were yelled out. Rather, it sounds like a friendly warning, like some advice given in the tone of someone who doesn't expect to be listened to, nor, in the end, who has that much desire to be heard. So the tourist, or whoever else happens at that moment to be treading the pavement that every true Ferrarese avoids, usually continues on their way without giving any sign of having understood what they were being warned of.

But the customers of the Caffè della Borsa, as I've already said, understand it only too well.

As soon as the absent-minded outsider hoves into view, the hubbub of conversation is quelled. Eyes stare, the breath is cut short. Will that person, who has nearly arrived at the paving-stones where the shooting took place, realize that he's about to do something he'd be much better leaving undone? Will he or will he not finally lift his head out of the *Touring Guide*? But above all, at a given moment, will the aerial and absurd, sad and ironic voice of the invisible Pino Barilari descend from above, or will it not? Maybe yes. Maybe no.

Awaiting the outcome often has a quality of muscular contraction, no more or less than that which attends a sporting event whose result is especially uncertain.

'Whoa there!'

Suddenly, in everyone's mind's eye the image of the chemist at the upstairs apartment window materializes. So, this time, he's there, seated at the windowsill, on the lookout, with his thin, hairy, very white arms raised to point at the passer-by who hasn't noticed the glint of the field glasses above. Many of those hidden in the protective shadow of the portico experience vivid relief to be where they are, rather than out in the open, utterly exposed.

2.

There weren't many people in Ferrara in 1939, a year that was so decisive for the fate of Italy and the rest of the world, who could tell anything that wasn't merely general about him or his life: about, that is, the man seated in pyjamas on an armchair with his back resting on two big white cushions, whose insistent presence at the window overlooking Corso Roma began to be noticed in the summer of that year.

That he was the only son of Dr Francesco Barilari, who died in 1936 and bequeathed him one of the best pharmacies in the city, that, yes, was a fact known even to the children of the most recent generation. Many a time, as if weighing the future potential of each of them, would the ironic, penetrating gaze of the meditative and bony chemist, whom they'd nicknamed Weighing Scales, fall on these boys in the mornings as, running to school, they passed along the portico of the Caffè della Borsa while taking the last puffs on cigarette ends reduced to their most vestigial stubs. There was little else to add about him other than that he had been a respected Mason of the 33rd degree who, in the early days, had had some sympathy for Fascism, and from time immemorial had been a widower.

The information about the young Barilari, if someone thirty-one years old can be called young, didn't go much further than what has already been said. When, for example, in 1936, at the death of the old Mason, he was promptly seen to take up his post behind the counter of the pharmacy, the surprise had been general. Encased in his white coat, he served the customers with confidence, and let them call him 'Doctor'. So he'd been to university and actually completed the course! they murmured, amazed. 'But where? And when? Who had studied with him?'

There was new surprise and wonderment in the autumn of 1937, on the occasion of his sudden marriage to Anna Repetto, the blonde, seventeen-year-old daughter of a marshal in the Carabinieri, originally from Chiavari, but for some years stationed, with his family, in Ferrara.

She was quite a wild type, forever going on bike rides or to dances in the local clubs, and always followed, not only by long trains of her contemporaries, but also by the gaze of many older men who were admiring her development from afar. In short, she was a young woman who was very eye-catching and very much in the public eye, so that to have her whisked away from under their very noses by someone like Pino Barilari, all of them felt somewhat swindled, betrayed even.

And then, soon after the wedding, more heated gossip about Pino circulated, but much more, to tell the truth, about his very young bride.

The most feverish predictions had been made about her by many. To be noticed on a beach at the nearby Adriatic Riviera by some bigshot from somewhere exotic, who would fall in love with one look, then marry her; a film director, also bewitched by her graces, who would take her back to Rome to be a star . . . So how could they possibly forgive her for having given in to the temptation to settle down, and in that way? They accused her of pettiness, of petit-bourgeois greed, of innate whorishness. They even taxed her with ingratitude to her family. Oh yes. Ligurians, such moneygrubbers – who knows what disappointment they too had had to face, those poor folk! And then when on earth had they seen each other, the two of them, before they were married? Where had they met up? If theirs hadn't been one of those worthless affairs, common enough, conducted by telephone, they would surely have been surprised every now and then in the vicinity of Piazza della Certosa, or along the bastions, or in Piazza d'Armi, and so on. So once again that sly operator Pino Barilari had acted with incredible flair. Hidden away in his pharmacy, he'd let the others, out there, wear themselves out in contemplation of Anna, who, with her blonde hair thrown back over her shoulders, with her generous lips all bright with lipstick, and, displaying up to her thighs and even further, her long, suntanned legs, would parade back and forth in front of the little tables of the Caffè della Borsa. Then just at the right moment, *snap*, he'd pulled in his net, and tough luck to the rest of them. Besides, was there really any need for him to be seen about with a free and unconstrained girl like Anna Repetto – a girl the city never lost sight of for a moment – if above the pharmacy, after the death of his father, he had an entire apartment at his disposal? Who would ever have noticed her if, say, she had discreetly entered the pharmacy at two in the afternoon, when no one would still be sitting under the awning of the Caffè della Borsa? A distasteful story, they concluded with a grimace, and decidedly vulgar. Since things ended as they did, better not to speak any more about it, better to just forget it.

Only the sudden paralysis that no more than two years later deprived Pino Barilari of the use of his legs had had the power once more to concentrate public attention on him. The result was to suspend him high up there, as in a royal box, a half-bust in pyjamas above the animated theatre of Corso Roma. From then on, his young wife, though of course for a while commiserated with, was barely considered. The conversations turned back to Pino, and to him alone. But wasn't it exactly this that he had sought, exhibiting himself as he did to the eyes of the world? And in fact he was always there now, seated from morning to evening at the window of the apartment above the pharmacy, and ready to glare at anyone who risked passing by within range along the pavement by the Castle moat, in a manner, as those same passers-by claimed, that was both insolent and unabashed. And happy as well! – they would add – as though it were the syphilis itself, which for so many years had lain meekly slumbering in his blood, and had at last broken out to

Within the Walls

deprive him of his legs, that had transformed his colourless life into something clear, comprehensible to him, in short *existent*. Now he felt strong, one could see it, even reborn; however, now he was utterly different from that kind of shipwrecked figure grabbing on to a lifebelt who, soon after the marriage, had on two or three occasions towards evening been seen arm in arm with his wife along the Giovecca. 'You see, my dear fellows, what a small youthful indiscretion can lead to?' he'd had the air of saying. 'This is what, can't you see?' In his now shining eyes there was no shadow to be seen. Of any kind.

But fully to understand the embarrassment, the instinctive suspicion, that this sort of behaviour induced in the townsfolk, it's worth at this point dwelling on the sense of stupor, uncertainty and general diffidence which had begun to diffuse itself throughout Italy, but especially in Ferrara, from the start of the summer of 1939.

In the eyes of many good people the city had at a stroke transformed itself into a kind of hell.

To begin with, there was the affair of those upper-school pupils, which kept cropping up in conversation – of that group of boys, none of them older than eighteen, who, prompted by their philosophy teacher, a certain Roccella – he had fled to Switzerland – had arrived at the sterling plan of smashing the windows, one each night, of the most important shops in the city centre, with the precise intent to foment panic and disorder among the population. This had meant that for the police to be able to lie in wait and catch the villains red-handed, their numbers had to be swollen by a score of old squad members, personally arranged into voluntary patrols by Carlo Aretusi, the renowned veteran Fascist who had joined up even before the March on Rome. Youthful high jinks they might have been, but regardless of the arrested boys' spirited professions of communism, the *Organizzazione per la Vigilanza e la Repressione dell'Antifascismo*[17] itself was involved in trying to downplay their political significance, and yet an element of that undoubtedly lingered. Things got worse, and that's for sure. Defeatists,

---

17 See the footnote about this organization on p. 80.

saboteurs and spies were lurking everywhere. That things were not going in the right direction could be read in the faces of certain Jews, for instance, who even then might be encountered in plain sight along Corso Roma, under the portico of the Caffè della Borsa – the whole lot of them ought to be shut up again in the ghettoes, and be done with the usual inappropriate pieties! – or it could be read in the faces of some of the city's more fanatical anti-Fascists who would pass by the Caffè della Borsa only on occasions of public calamities, and these befell us almost every day: there they were, always there, just like other birds of ill-omen of a similar plume. Only the blind would be unaware of the malicious pleasure that, from under the habitual mask of indifference, issued from their every pore! Only the deaf would not have heard in the voice with which the honourable Bottecchiari, seated some way off, hailed the waiter Giovanni to order his usual aperitif – a strong, calm, crisply articulate voice, which made the customers across the whole locale jump – the derision of someone already looking forward to and savouring their revenge! And what could it mean, that absurd mania to display himself that had seized hold of Pino Barilari, if not that, as an anti-Fascist, a subversive, he too wanted to expedite the defeat of the nation? In his open display of an unseemly disease wasn't it possible to descry a subtly offensive and provocative intent, beside which, even the fourteen shop windows left shattered from the stones thrown by the so-called 'gang of pupils', was footling child's play?

These worries spread abroad and reached the upper echelons.

Yet despite these things, when asked his opinion by the select court of his most faithful followers that encircled him, Carlo Aretusi, nicknamed Sciagura, drew down his mouth in an expression of doubt.

'Don't let's exaggerate,' he replied with a smile.

In the inseparable company of Vezio Sturla and Osvaldo Bellistracci he had maintained his – you could call it permanent – station for, by now, twenty years, at the very same table of the Caffè della Borsa. And so it was to him, as the most authoritative member of what at the time of the 'action squads' had been Ferrara's famous

Within the Walls

Fascist triumvirate, that the most delicate questions were addressed without delay.

Sceptical, nostalgic, Sciagura kept on smiling. Despite the insistence of the others, he couldn't be induced to see that in Pino Barilari's behaviour there was anything at all threatening.

'That draft dodger a subversive?' he finally blurted out, laughing. 'If you'd been with us in Rome in 1922!'

Thus it was – it's worth recording because this had never happened before – that from the lips of Sciagura, twisted for the occasion into an emotional grimace, the little group of his confidants were able to hear him tell with a remarkable abundance of detail *also* about the March on Rome.

Ah yes, Sciagura sighed. He, unlike certain others, was always reluctant to speak at all about the March on Rome!

Why – he continued at once, with emphasis – why ever would he waste his time chattering about an event like that, which if for many it had meant the seizure of power, with all the consequent personal advantages accrued, for him, as for others like him – and here Sturla and Bellistracci nodded in silent confirmation – it represented one thing only: the end of the revolution, the definitive eclipse of the glorious era of the squads?

And then, when you considered the matter closely, what was it if not a kind of military convoy making for the capital, with stops at all the stations, to gather the platoons of comrades-in-arms (from Bologna to Florence, in those days, the tunnels made for the fast trains weren't yet even dreamt of), and a proper troop of armed Carabinieri and Royal Guards placed as protection along the whole line? Fat chance that they'd be there to guard the four Fiat 18 BLs which, in 1919, had pushed as far forward as Molinella, deep into the Red zone, to set fire to the HQ of the Workers' Organization. That was some feat – which, for the first time, had drawn all of Italy's attention to the Fascist Federation of Ferrara, and which, to be precise, led to the very first friction between the Ferrara and the Bologna federations, as the latter had considered – and explicitly called – the Molinella expedition a 'provocative interference'. Fascism was at that time anarchic, Garibaldi-like. Then, as opposed to later, bureaucrats were not preferred to revolutionaries. But in 1919 or '20 the young Sciagura, the young Bellistracci, the young Sturla, armed only with clubs, with knuckledusters or, at the most, with some old SIPE-manufactured hand-grenades left over from the war, would leave by night from Porta Reno looking for a fight with the Communist dockers who crowded the drinking dens of Borgo San Luca – it had actually been them, the Bolshevik workers from beyond Porta Reno, who had nicknamed him Sciagura: and he had always boasted of the name, and had always worn it like a medal for bravery. No way were they counting on any assistance, even of an indirect kind, from the police! It wasn't until 1922, or rather '23, that the police began to give a hand to the Fascists. In that later period, before setting out on any punitive raid, they used to assemble with all the trucks and cars in the Castle's central courtyard. After 1923, the farm owners from outside might also have been seen, rushing to offer their cars, declaring themselves highly honoured to put them at the service of the Cause!

But getting back to the March on Rome and the son of Dr Barilari – in the end it was him, the boy, who provided the only real entertainment for the whole trip. Thinking back, it was actually he who salvaged the March on Rome.

He had joined them at the last moment, when the train was already leaving, so a hand had to be stretched from the window to haul him up like a deadweight. The way he was dressed! He was wearing a grey-green cloak which must have been his father's and reached down to his hocks, military puttees which slipped on his legs every five minutes, big, low-cut, yellow shoes, and in addition a great fez, which, crushed down on his head, made his ears stick out like a bat's. What could you do, seeing yourselves gawped at by his idiot eyes on stalks, but split your sides with laughter? It seemed like the boy thought that he, Sciagura, was a kind of Tom Mix and that the others in the 'hand-grenade' squad had been the sheriff's posse. 'Who are you? Not by chance Dr Barilari's son?' someone had soon asked. Without being able to reply, he was so out of breath, he'd nodded in the affirmative. 'But does your daddy know you've sneaked away with us?' He shook his head for No, all the while staring at them with his baby eyes as if he'd been dropped into a cowboy film.

At eighteen years old, he was far from being a kid. But he was worse than a kid.

At that age he was still a virgin. Since the train, on the way there as on the way back, stopped at more or less every station, and they made the most of nearly every stop by going in search of brothels, and he, Pino, always stubborn as a mule, refused to set foot inside any of them, it ended up with them hauling him in by force. He resisted, dragged his feet, pleaded with his hands together and wept. 'What're you so scared of – d'you think they're going to eat you?' the others said. 'At least come in and have a look. Word of honour we won't make you go upstairs into any of the bedrooms!'

He didn't believe us. At a certain moment he, Sciagura, smiling and winking, intervened and took him aside, and whispered something in his ear. 'D'you really not want to come in?' he said. 'Go on, stop playing the fool!'

Only then did he decide to go in, even if then, as soon as he'd entered the salon with all the others, he huddled down in a corner all on his own. The girls, egged on and touched by him being so scared – it should be said they always had a weakness for Fascists! – were all in competition to pet him; you can't imagine what lengths they went to. Listening to him, you'd think those girls had turned the brothel into a home for abandoned children. And sure enough the madam came in to sort things out. 'Now what's going on here, girls?' she yelled at them. 'Are we running a wet-flannel factory?' Every time they stopped off, it was a comedy, a farce of this kind.

The mother of all scenes happened at Specchi, a brothel in Bologna, on the return journey.

Given that the Porrettana line[18] was never-ending – they'd been bored to death on the way there – at Pistoia, before they had to cope with the Apennines, they'd got out in twos and threes to buy up all the flasks of Chianti they could get their hands on. Up in the mountains it gets cold, and so misty you can't see ten metres ahead. To

18 The Porrettana railway line runs from Pistoia to Rome, over 300 kilometres.

pass the time, there was nothing to do but drink and sing songs, the result being that when they arrived at Bologna towards midnight, all of them, Pino included, were completely drunk.

At the end of Via dell'Oca, pressing his back against the knocker made of nail-heads on the small entrance door, Pino once again started going through his usual rigmarole of resistance. It was then, that he, Sciagura, perhaps because of the alcohol, or the boredom of the journey, or the anger at having taken part in that great travesty that was the March on Rome – at Rome, they'd stayed barely a couple of days, for most of that time stuck in the barracks and never getting even a glimpse of Il Duce, because, they said, he was haggling with the king about forming a government – anyway, suddenly, without knowing quite how, he found himself with the Mauser in his fist pointed at the boy's throat, saying that if Pino didn't stop whining and go in right away, or even, when they'd gone in to the little salon upstairs, if he refused to go up to a room with a prostitute, he'd have to face a lot worse than syphilis. As things turned out, it was probably then that he actually did catch it!

It had been he who accompanied the boy upstairs, to make sure that the two of them did their business and that properly. Lucky Pino had done as he was told! If he hadn't, then he, Sciaguro, drunk as he was and levelling that revolver at him, well, anything might have happened.

3.

Who in Ferrara does not remember the night of 15 December, 1943? Who could forget the slow creep of the hours that night? For everyone it was an anxious, interminable vigil, with burning eyes peering through the slats of blinds at streets cloaked in the darkness of a blackout, and the heart leaping every minute at the crackle of machine-gun fire or the sudden passing, even noisier, of the trucks packed with armed men.

> Death holds for us no fear,
> Long live death and the cemetery . . .

sang the unseen men in the trucks. It was a cadenced, rather than warlike song, but that lilt, too, was full of desperation.

News of the assassination of Consul Bolognesi, the ex-Federal Secretary (who, since September, after the interval of the Badoglio period, had been called upon to reorganize the Fascist Federation and assume its governership), had spread around the city in the early afternoon of the 15th. A little later, the radio supplied the details: the Topolino car found on a country road near Copparo, the left-side window wide open; the victim with his head slumped on the steering wheel 'as though sleeping'; the 'classic' shot to the back of the neck, 'more telling than a signature'; and the contempt, 'the unstoppable tide of contempt', which the news, as soon as it was received, had provoked in Verona, in the heart of the Constituent Assembly of the New Social Republic assembled in Castelvecchio. Towards evening, it was possible to hear a live recording from the session in Verona. A thin, high voice had suddenly taken over from the deep, sorrowful voice of the speaker, who, having informed the listeners of the death of Consul Bolognesi, had begun to fashion his eulogy, shouting angrily and sorrowfully like a child throwing a tantrum: 'We shall avenge our comrade, Bolognesi!' The radios were switched off, people stared at each other with frightened expressions, and already the dull rumbling of distant tanks approaching and the lacerating *rat-a-tat* of the first bursts of machine-gun fire could be heard outside.

No one went to bed, no one even thought of sleeping. There wasn't, in short, a single person in Ferrara who didn't fear that their house would be raided. But it was above all in the city's middle-class apartments that feverish discussions and arguments raged.

What was happening? What would happen now?

It's true, they reasoned, seated torpidly around those same tables, the tablecloths still covered with crumbs and only half-cleared of the lunch's dirty dishes, on which, at a given time as on every other evening, they were vainly attempting to eat supper – it's true that the city was resounding with the noise of gunfire, with lugubrious songs that spoke of death and cemeteries. But this shouldn't make them think that the Fascists, who, even in Ferrara, confining themselves since that September to rounding up the hundred or so Jews they'd managed to get their hands on and a mere ten anti-Fascists, locking them up in Piangipane Prison, had, all considered, shown remarkable moderation, now, having suddenly switched tactics and, beginning in the city itself, wanted to bring about a general and radical turn of the screw. Good Lord, they might be Fascists, but they were also Italians! And, to tell the truth, a lot more Italian than many others who liked to expatiate on Freedom while polishing the shoes of the foreign invader. No, surely there was nothing to fear. If the Fascists were kicking up a bit of a fuss, swaggering about looking fierce, with skulls on their berets, they were doing it mainly to keep at bay the Germans, who, left to themselves, wouldn't have hesitated to treat Italy like some kind of Poland or Ukraine. What poor devils the Fascists were! You had to understand the predicament they were in, and the personal tragedy of Mussolini, poor fellow too, who, if he hadn't yet retired from public life to the Rocca delle Caminate, his summer residence, as he perhaps hoped to, that would only have been because of Italy's dire plight. But the king, the king! On 8 September, all the king could do, along with Badoglio, was cut the cord. By contrast, in the hour of crisis, Mussolini, as a good Romagnolo (the Savoy royal family and Badoglio were Piedmontese, and the Piedmontese had always been a stingy, untrustworthy lot!), hadn't hesitated for an instant to wade into the waves, rush up the gangplank and grab the tiller ... And frankly, how should the assassination of the Consul Bolognesi be judged – a paterfamilias, besides, and a man who'd never harmed a hair on anyone's head? No true Italian could approve of a crime like that, which was, it was obvious, like a servile imitation of Yugoslavia or France, so as to spread the flames and all the horrors of a partisan war into Italy too. The destruction of all the finest Western and Mediterranean values: in short, communism – that's the real aim of a partisan war! If the Yugoslavs and the French, despite the recent experience of Spain, wanted communism, well, they had their Tito

Within the Walls

and their De Gaulle. For Italians today, as things were, there was a single obligation: to stay united and save what could be saved.

Finally, and mercifully, daylight returned. And with the light, the songs and shooting ceased.

And at the same time, at a stroke, the nervous chattering behind doors and windows ceased. But the anxiety did not abate. Daylight, restoring even to the blindest an exact sense of reality, made it even more acute. What did that sudden silence portend? What was it hiding or preparing? It could easily be a trap fashioned to trick people into coming out so that they could then be rounded up. Before any vague news of the massacre had gradually spread, as if by its own momentum, they stayed cooped up inside their houses for at least two hours.

The victims of the reprisal were fifty, a hundred, two hundred. If the most desperate predictions were to be given any credit, not just Corso Roma, but the whole city centre would be strewn with corpses.

And yet there were only eleven, laid in three separate heaps along the wall of the Castle moat, on that stretch of pavement exactly opposite the Caffè della Borsa. To count and identify them, which was done by the first who dared approach – from a way off they didn't even look like human bodies: rags, poor rags at that, or bundles thrown there in the sun and the dirty melting snow – it was necessary to turn those that lay face down over on to their backs and separate, one from the other, those who fell embracing each other and had become a tight tangle of rigid limbs. There was only just time to count and recognize them. Because soon after, emerging from the corner of Giovecca, a small military van came to a halt with a theatrical screech of brakes in front of the group who had gathered around the bodies. 'Away! Move away!' the Black Brigade militia who were riding in the van yelled out. Still pursued by their shouts, nothing remained for those who were present but slowly to retreat towards the two ends of Corso Roma, and from there, under the sun now already high, their eyes still on the four militia men down there who kept guard over the dead with machine-guns in their hands, to let the whole city know by telephone what they'd risked and what they'd seen.

Horror, pity, crazed fear: all of these were mingled in the impression which the announcement of the names of the dead awoke in every household. There were only eleven of them, agreed. But they were persons only too well known in Ferrara, persons about whom, beyond their names, a surfeit of details both physical and moral were only too familiar for their end not to appear from the first a terrifying event, of an almost incredible brutality. It will seem strange that the nearly unanimous abhorrence of the murder could at once be accompanied by an equally widespread intention to treat the murderers respectfully, to make a public show of supporting and submitting to their violence. Yet this is what happened, and it would be futile to try to conceal the fact, if it's true, as it was, that in no other city of northern Italy could the Fascism that was reborn in Verona have then been able to count on such a large number of enrolled Party members as might be seen on the morning of the 17th in long, silent queues in the courtyard of the Fascist headquarters in Viale Cavour waiting for the Federation offices to open. Bent, submissive, disheartened under the worn-out greatcoats made of autarchic fabrics, they were the same silent tide of people who, the afternoon of the day before, had step by step followed the coffin of Consul Bolognesi along Corso Giovecca, Via Palestro, Via Borso, up to the Piazza della Certosa, and in whose leaden features the few who had remained inside their houses to watch the cortège from behind their blinds had, with a shudder, been able to recognize their own faces. What else was there to do but give in? The Germans and Japanese, even if for the moment they seemed in retreat, would reverse the situation, uncovering an arsenal of secret weapons of unheard-of power, and win the war with a lightning strike. No, there was only one road left to take.

But those who committed the massacre, who were they? The whole city had started to wonder since the day after. There was no doubt: the first perpetrators, those materially responsible for the massacre, could be none other than the men from the military cars, four of them with licence plates 'VR', from Verona, and two 'PD', from Padua – the same ones that throughout the night had filled Ferrara with their songs and firing, and then, towards dawn, had disappeared. The avengers predicted by the radio had certainly been them. And in fact it was they, the squad members from the Veneto, who presented themselves at the entrance of the prison in Via Piangipane, and it was they, and they alone, who, with guns in their hands, had forced that poor chap, the director, to hand over the lawyers Polenghi and Tamagnini, both of them Socialists and veteran trade union organizers, and also the lawyers Galimberti, Fano and Forlivesi of the *Partito d'Azione*,[19] all of them detained since September, all awaiting investigation.

And yet, to belie the rumour which was already circulating, according to which no Ferrarese had participated in the atrocity, no Ferrarese was stained with that blood, it was quite enough to ponder the other six dead, National Councillor Abbove, Dr Malacarne, the accountant Zoli, the two Cases, father and son, and the worker Felloni, at least five of whom were taken from their own houses. Apart from Felloni, a little-known employee of the Electric Company, who had been rounded up with the group of victims only because a little before dawn, the hour at which he usually went to work, he'd happened to run into one of the patrols which were blocking the way to the city centre, no one who wasn't from Ferrara – a point argued by many – could possibly have been able to track down National Councillor Abbove, who was not then in his home in Corso Giovecca, but in the office-*garçonnière*, which, having bought the site within a narrow medieval cloister very cheaply, he had recently had built in the quiet and secluded Via Brasàvola, and in whose discreet shade, filled with the most various of art objects, the old epicure was wont to repair, on certain afternoons, to enjoy his declining years. No one who wasn't from the city (very well informed indeed about what had been going on there over the last years) could possibly have known of the secret meetings which, during the forty-five days of the Badoglio period, had been held in that big trap belonging to the National Councillor Abbove. Dr Malacarne and the accountant Zoli had always attended, but old Sciagura, no – he had declined each and every invitation. These

---

19 For information about this political party, see the footnote on p. 97.

meetings were thought to have been to work out a strategy for all those Fascists who, with the fall of the regime, only wanted to send word to the king, attesting to their 'unconditional loyalty' – in short, to change their views as swiftly as a weathervane. And the two Cases, father and son, especially, two of the few Jews to have escaped from the big round-up in September, leather merchants who had never had a political thought in their lives and had lived, since September, hidden away in the barn of their old house in Vicolo Mozzo Torcicoda, and had been provided with food through a hole in the floor by their wife and mother, respectively, who was as Aryan and Catholic as could be ... who else but someone who had the most intimate knowledge of their place of refuge could have been able to point the four cut-throats sent to capture them just there, atop that dusty labyrinth of half-crumbled little staircases? Who else but ...?

Carlo Aretusi, yes, him, Sciagura. As to why suspicion should immediately have alighted on his person (since the morning of the 16th he had resumed command of the Federation, and his name was spoken henceforth as it had been before 1922 in an instinctively hushed tone), it's enough to recall how he had appeared at the funeral of Consul Bolognesi on the afternoon of that day.

He had never participated in the many clandestine meetings which in August had been held at the house of National Councillor Abbove, even sending word to his ex-comrades that he, not wanting to renege at fifty on what he had done at twenty years of age, had no wish to attend. And so, while he walked at the head of the interminable cortège just in front of the gun carriage which bore the coffin of Consul Bolognesi and kept casting glances of scorn and hatred in the direction of the houses in Corso Giovecca and in Via Palestro – how free and easy he seemed, wearing, despite the cold, only his black shirt with his beret of the Tenth Assault Flotilla, disbanded in 1923, his temples only just beginning to turn grey – he seemed to be exactly as he'd been as a young man at twenty. 'Damned vermin, cowardly, boot-licking bourgeoisie! I'll show you! I'll flush you all out!' his furious eyes and curled lips seemed to be threatening. In Piazza della Certosa, before the coffin was borne into the church, he had harangued the crowd in this very tone. Grey and inert, the crowd listened. He seemed to become more and more infuriated, perhaps most of all infuriated because of that inertia.

'The bodies of the eleven traitors shot in Corso Roma at dawn this morning,' he had yelled in conclusion, 'won't be removed until I give the order. We want to be sure that their example will have the desired effect!'

In that paroxysm of rage could he have boasted any more explicitly of having administered justice himself, with his own hands?

A little after, in Corso Roma, when he had unexpectedly arrived to call to attention the Black Brigade militia, who were guarding the bodies of the slain, how should one interpret his behaviour, which seemed so at odds with that of a half-hour earlier in Piazza della Certosa, except that, reconsidering, it added up to more than a hundred confessions?

Sullenly he got out of the car, barely sparing a glance at the corpses stretched out on the pavement, and at once one of the soldiers took a step forwards to inform him, with the air of congratulating him for having arrived at the right moment, of all that had been happening.

The whole day, the militia man explained, speaking on behalf of himself and his companions, the three of them had managed to keep at bay anyone who had tried to approach. More than once, with the aim of dispersing them – they were most likely the traitors' relatives, women weeping and crying out, men who were swearing; it wasn't in the least bit easy to make them obey! – they'd been forced to fire a few bursts of bullets into the air to drive them off down there to the far corners of the Piazza Cattedrale and Corso Giovecca, where even now, as Comrade Aretusi could see, a few of them still seemed determined to stay. But what else could they have done – the soldier went on and, raising his arm, pointed to the window, behind which one could make out the motionless shape of Pino Barilari – about that gentleman up there, a really weird guy, I can tell you, when no hint or threat, no burst of machine-gun fire has made him budge an inch? Who knows, perhaps he was deaf? Still, if they'd known how to reach him, even if it meant breaking through the shutters down there in the pharmacy, one of them would surely have gone up to tell him from close up, politely or otherwise, to move the hell away . . .

As soon as the soldier had said 'that gentleman up there', Sciagura, with a start as though he'd been bitten by an adder, had raised his eyes to the window the young man was pointing at. It was dark by then. Seeping up over the rim of the Castle moat, minute by minute, the fog was thickening. Along the whole length of Corso Roma that window up there was the only one lit.

Still looking up at it, Sciagura let out a stifled curse and gave a scornful gesture. He then turned round, and in a muffled voice, a kind of timorous murmur, ordered the three soldiers, in some twenty minutes' time, when the men he had sent to remove the bodies arrived, to let them do it, and not to get in their way.

4.

People imagined things.

They imagined entering the apartment above the pharmacy, where no one from Ferrara, not even the Freemason brothers of the deceased Francesco, had ever even once set foot. A little spiral staircase linked the back workroom to the upstairs floor, which consisted of only four rooms: a dining-room, a drawing-room, a double bedroom and finally the little room which Pino had had as a boy, and to which, since being struck down by paralysis, he'd once again returned . . . By the sheer effort of imagining it, it was as though they had come to know the apartment intimately – to the extent of being able to point to the very wall on which hung the portrait photograph of Weighing Scales in a heavy, gilded, nineteenth-century frame, and to describe the shape of the central chandelier which every evening cast its strong, white light over the table's green cover and on the cards of the game of patience, or to tell of the effect of the modern furniture and objects, scattered here and there, but mostly in the double bedroom, which had been introduced by the young Signora Barilari, or to expound on the little room adjoining the bedroom where, soon after supper, Pino retired to sleep,

Within the Walls

with a child's iron bed in one corner, a small desk against one wall, a wardrobe against the opposite wall, and at the foot of the bed, covered with a blanket of Scottish wool in red-and-blue tartan, the big armchair with adjustable back which every morning his wife replaced beside the light-filled dining-room window, and on which Pino sat from morning to evening. If they'd wanted to they could even have listed one by one the authors shelved in the glass-fronted bookcase next to the radiator beside the door – Salgari, Verne, Ponson du Terrail, Dumas, Mayne Reid, Fenimore Cooper, and so on. Among the other books there was also *The Narrative of Arthur Gordon Pym* by E. A. Poe, in an edition whose cover depicted a tall white ghost armed with a sickle looming over a little whaling sloop. Yet this latter volume was not behind the glass of the bookcase alongside the other books, but, rather, face down on the bedside table's shelf beside a fat stamp album, a bundle of crayons upright behind a glass, a cheap penknife, a half-consumed eraser; the volume placed, then, so that the spectre on the cover, while still being present, *being there*, was invisible, and did not arouse any fear.

But this wasn't enough.

'Where are you going?' Pino had asked on the evening of 15 December, raising his head from a game of patience.

Having got up from the table, his wife Anna was already moving towards the door. And it was from the shadowy corridor, at the end of which the trapdoor opened on to the spiral staircase, that her calm voice reached him in reply.

'Where d'you think I'm going? I'm going down to close the shop.'

Who knows? Perhaps he hadn't heard on the radio, early that afternoon, the report from Verona. What is certain is that at nine o'clock, when the chimes of the Castle clock had faded over the whole city with the slow sweetness of a benediction, one would have expected Pino to be huddled up in his child's bed, the covers drawn up to his ears. Closing his eyes, going to sleep. Hearing his wife get up from the table to go down to the pharmacy – at that hour there was always something to do down there: tot up the day's earnings and, finally, having drawn down the shutters, to lock up from inside – and seeing her about to leave through the drawing-room door, so tall and beautiful and indifferent, what would Pino be thinking about except that? To fall into a deep sleep. And that evening, perhaps, even earlier than usual.

They also imagined everything else, naturally, everything else that happened.

They saw the eleven men lined up in three distinct groups against the little wall of the Castle moat, the coming and going of the blue-shirted legionnaires in that space between the portico of the Caffè della Borsa and the opposite pavement, the desperate sneer of the lawyer Fano, when, an instant before the firing began, he had shouted 'Murderer!' at Sciagura, who was standing a little apart lighting a cigarette, that clear light, that incredibly clear moonlight which, since midnight, with the wind's sudden change, had made every stone of the city a piece of glass or coal, and Pino, finally, whom only the cry of the lawyer Fano had managed to drag at the last moment from his childlike deep sleep, hidden up there, shaking on his crutches, behind the windowpanes which overlooked the scene ... And it was thus, for months and months, the whole time it took from December 1943 to May '44 for the war to slowly advance up the Italian peninsula, as if the collective imagination needed to return to that spot, to that fearful night, and to have before its eyes the faces of the eleven men who were shot just as Pino had seen them from his lofty vantage-point.

The Liberation came, and finally Peace, and for many Ferrarese, for almost all of them, came the anxious need to forget.

But can one forget? Is it enough to want to?

In the summer of 1946, when in the conference room of the ex-Fascist HQ in Viale Cavour the trial began of the twenty or so presumed perpetrators of the massacre of three years earlier (most of them from the Veneto, collared in the Coltano concentration camp and the prisons), and when, hiding under a false name in the refuge in Colle Val d'Elsa where he had been tracked down by the young and very active provincial secretary of the *Associazione Nazionale Partigiani d'Italia*,[20] Nino Bottecchiari, Sciagura too made his entry into the big cage, the dock of the accused, this seemed the most auspi-

20 See footnote on p. 69.

cious occasion finally to place a covering stone over the past. It was, however, true, they sighed, that no other city in northern Italy had supplied as many adherents to the Republic of Salò as Ferrara had, no other middle class had been so ready to kowtow to the dismal banners of its various militia and special corps. And yet it would have needed very little indeed for that error of calculation which many had made under the pressure of such exceptional circumstances, and which the Communists of the region, taking control of the town hall in 1945, had tended to turn into a stain of eternal infamy, for that simple, only human error to become along with everything else just a bad dream, a terrible nightmare from which to awake full of hope, faith in themselves and in the future! Sufficient to this end would have been the condemnation of the assassins, and then every memory of that night of 15 December 1943, that fatal, decisive night, could be rapidly and finally erased.

The trial inched forward in the heat and boredom, provoking in the jostling crowd which gathered for every sitting a growing sense of futility and impotence.

Made restless and uneasy by the loudspeakers placed in the avenue outside which broadcast the proceedings as far away as the city centre, as the middle of Corso Roma, the court interrogated the accused one by one. From behind the bars of the big cage placed along one side of the courtroom, between two windows, the accused kept responding in the same way: none of them had been involved in the punitive expedition of December 1943; none of them had even been to Ferrara. They all seemed so sure they had nothing to fear that some of them even risked the odd joke. There was one from Treviso, for example, with long curly dark hair and a jutting, unshaven jaw, who admitted that, yes, he had in fact once been to Ferrara, but twenty years earlier, on a bike to meet his girlfriend – a joke which didn't fail to elicit a sly and good-natured, typically Neapolitan grin from the presiding judge, who always seemed inclined to distance himself from that aura of populist, revolutionary justice the trial had begun to assume. If he had allowed the sittings to take place in the ex-Fascist HQ – so he had said on the first day – it was only because the courthouse, half-destroyed by a bombardment in 1944 and in the process of reconstruction, was still unfit for use.

As for Sciagura, not only did he too deny any direct or indirect involvement in the 'event' of 15 December 1943, but from the first moment that the Carabinieri put him in the cage, he never lost an opportunity to display, along with the most punctilious respect for the court called to judge his 'actions', his deep disdain for the crowd down in the public space, whose behaviour, he said at a certain point, revealed only too clearly the baleful effect 'of the present state of affairs'. So was it, he added, with factional hatred, with the thirst for revenge that could be seen on all those faces that the much hoped-for national pacification was to be achieved? Was this the climate of freedom to enable the court to pass a cool and unprejudiced judgement on a man like him, only guilty of having been 'a soldier in the service of an Idea'?

All this was merely blowing smoke in the eyes of the court, evasive tactics meant to delay and to stop the proceedings from becoming too legalistic, which would be to his disadvantage, whereas a political trial could only work in his favour.

'I was the foot soldier of an Idea,' he kept repeating in a self-pleased way, 'not the system's hired assassin nor the servant of foreign powers!'

Or in a maudlin tone: 'Everyone now speaks ill of me!'

He didn't need to add anything more. But each time it was as though he hinted that his persecutors of today shouldn't fool themselves that condemning him would draw a veil over what they themselves had been yesterday. Every one of them had been just as much a Fascist as him, and no court verdict was going to wipe away that fact.

And in the end what was it he was being accused of? he said, going on the offensive one day. If he'd not misunderstood, he was accused of having supplied the list of eleven persons who were shot on the night of 15 December 1943, and of having personally directed the execution of those 'unfortunates'. But to convince a 'proper', a 'responsible' court that he, Carlo Aretusi, had really done those two things, proffered the list and directed the execution, proof was required – not mere suppositions! 'There's no point in chattering about the slaughter, since I myself am ready to assume full and complete responsibility for it!' It seemed he'd declared as much some days after the 'famous night', and it may indeed be that, on that or on another occasion, those had been his words. And so? Once again, proof is required, proof! As for the sentences he may have spoken then, 'in the heat of the moment', they were 'in all probability' intended to assure 'our German allies' of the commitment and unconditional loyalty of Italy. After 8 September the Germans had become the real rulers of Italy, and, as we know, they wouldn't have had any hesitation in reducing every town in the land to a pile of rubble. So what counted wasn't words, and words, remember, spoken in public so that *others* might hear and heed them. What counted were facts and deeds, not to mention the medals for valour that he, during the First World War, had won fighting against those very Germans to whom he was now accused of being a lackey – he, a lackey? – a stormtrooper on the Piave! And since the stockholders of the Agricola Bank had been referred to, why not also remember that the honourable Bottecchiari, the Socialist lawyer Mauro Bottecchiari, who until the fall of the 'Badoglio government' had served on the board of directors of that bank, had been released at Christmas from the Via Piangipane prison due to his, Carlo Aretusi's, direct intervention? Also the schoolmistress Trotti, another Socialist, had been set free on the same occasion, and it's a shame that now she's no longer with us to testify on his behalf. But the honourable Bottecchiari is still enjoying the best of health. So why not call on him at once and ask him to relate all that he knows of the matter? The honourable Bottecchiari is a good man, utterly trustworthy and above any pettiness, and for this reason he, Sciagura, had always had the utmost respect for him since the remote times of 1920, and '22. The truth is that compared to how things were once, nowadays everywhere in Italy political conduct has massively deteriorated! Another truth ought to be told: that today they wanted to condemn Carlo Aretusi mainly because he had been 'promoted' to lead the federal Fascist secretariat of Ferrara on the day after Consul Bolognesi's assassination. For a reason of this kind, of 'scheming politics' today, they wanted to make a scapegoat of Carlo Aretusi. A 'proper' court, a 'responsible' court, a court that wouldn't let itself be 'swayed by factional prejudices' would at once have understood that he had accepted the directorship with the exclusive aim of hindering certain 'lawless desperadoes' from instigating a reign of terror. And, in fact, what had been the first step he had taken as soon as he was appointed but to restore without delay the bodies of the victims to their respective families?'

Every now and then, to be fair, the presiding judge would remember to interrupt him, mildly calling him to order, and he, for his part, always showed himself ready to let go of the bars of the cage, which he kept gripping hold of while he spoke, to desist from giving fiery looks towards the public space at the end of the court, and to sit back down on the bench alongside the other accused. But these concessions of his lasted a very short time. At the first phrase from the public prosecutor that displeased him, or at any witness's testimony that he considered 'erroneous' or at the slightest murmur from the public, or, most of all, at the tiniest hint made about his active participation in the shooting on the night of 15 December 1943, he would once more spring to his feet, wildly grab hold of the bars of the cage, and again raise his heavy, grating voice, the voice of an old commander, which the loudspeakers outside broadcast in a wide arc across the city.

'Let's see the witnesses!' he yelled like a madman. 'Let's see who has the guts to say such a thing to my face!'

Yet he suddenly fell silent when he saw Pino Barilari in person, making his way through the crowd, holding with one hand the arm of his wife, with the other a big, knotty, rubber-tipped walking stick; his legs in baggy, seroual breeches were thin as twigs and moved in a strange lateral sweep with the effort of walking.

From that moment on, as though hypnotized, he neither moved nor took his eyes off the chemist, for whom, as well as for his wife, Nino Bottecchiari, never absent from the courtroom, hurriedly found a space in the section reserved for the witnesses – it had been him, besides, who had suggested in a letter to the court that the paralysed man be called as a witness. Sciagura actually did move, but only very slowly, to keep smoothing down his iron-grey hair with his right hand. At the same time, he was thinking – you could see it in his face – he didn't stop thinking for a moment.

At last it was Pino Barilari's turn to take the stand.

Still supported by his wife, he came forwards and was duly sworn in, though he was barely audible.

But in the second before he answered the presiding judge's question and pronounced with almost pedantic clarity the brief phrase 'I was sleeping', which like a pin bursting a balloon filled with air had shrivelled to nothing the huge tension that held the entire court – the silence was absolute, no one breathed and even his wife leant anxiously forwards to scrutinize his face – in that second, quite a few observers distinctly saw Sciagura give Pino Barilari a rapid, propitiating grimace. And a wink of shared understanding, an almost imperceptible wink.

5.

For the last word to be said on this question, some further years had to pass. In the meantime everyone found a way of resuming their life. Pino Barilari began to pass the most part of his days sitting in front of his usual window once more, but he'd become embittered and ironic, with field glasses always within reach, and implacable in fulfilling the role he seemed to have assigned himself: of forever surveying the passers-by on that stretch of pavement below. And all the other, old habitués together with the next generation of youths (Sciagura, of course, included, since his trial had resulted in a full acquittal) had returned to share out between them the tables and chairs of the caffè beneath him.

In 1948, just after the elections of 18 April, Anna Barilari left her husband's house and at once began proceedings to obtain a legal separation. People assumed that she would return to live with her family in Marshal Repetto's house. But they were mistaken.

Instead she went to live alone in a little apartment at the end of the Giovecca, near the Prospettiva: two windows, encased in bulging ironwork that directly overlooked the pavement. And although she was now almost thirty years old, and, shapely though she still was, seemed even older, she once again began going for bike rides as she had as a girl, when she had attracted droves of school companions, and there were many in Ferrara who still remembered such things well.

Enrolled in the Drawing Academy in Via Romei, she wore low-necked pullovers which displayed her imposing bust, her long, mustard-blonde hair thrown back behind her, and used more make-up than ever. She probably aspired to the look of the existentialist young women of Paris and Rome. In reality, she was on the game, and no joke! – as those who should know attested, if their account was true – that she frequented the restaurants and cheap eating places of San Romano on Mondays with the evident aim of picking up a client among those who came to Ferrara for market day.

She would sometimes disappear, though, for periods that varied from one to as much as three weeks. When she popped up again it wasn't rare that she'd be accompanied by a woman, befriended who knows where, with whom, sometimes for a whole month, she'd be seen walking arm in arm up and down the streets, awakening ever-replenished ripples of interest round about. Who on earth was that brunette with the malicious eyes who was now with Anna? was asked everywhere. Was she by chance from Bologna? Or from Rome? And that other one there with the blue eyes, and the pale, refined features, the heelless and almost, it seemed, soleless shoes, was she from Florence, or, if not, from abroad?

On the same evening there was no shortage of men willing to trek to the end of the Giovecca to check up on these facts. Having reached the apartment occupied by Signora Barilari, they would discreetly tap on the windowpanes in winter so they could be let in, in summer simply to have a chat through the window from the pavement. So, in that vicinity, at some midnights in July or August it wasn't unusual to come across three or four men standing in a group, flirting with Anna or whatever friend she might have with her.

These were usually men between thirty and forty, not a few of whom had a wife and children. They had known Anna since she was a girl, and some of them had even been at school with her. As a result, later, around one or two in the morning, when they reappeared at the Caffè della Borsa and, hot and tired, with the sleeves of their linen jackets rolled up, slumped into the chairs, they would talk and tell stories chiefly about her until it was time to turn in.

She wasn't a straightforward character, Anna! they'd sigh.

It may well have been to do with the fact that until very recently she had been a respectable housewife, or else because they were ill-equipped to fathom certain mysteries of the female mind: the truth was that they never knew what tone to adopt. You could be talking away to her from the pavement and she'd suddenly slam the window in your face, and then a minute later open it again if, instead of shrugging and cursing her, you'd stayed and knocked on the window again and whistled. But it was the same old tune if you went inside. Afterwards, for example, it was never clear whether or not you ought to insist on her taking the thousand *lire*. And the long sentimental preludes you had to put up with? And the unease her continuous, endless, tireless chatter induced? While she was still getting dressed again, she'd resume talking about herself, about Pino Barilari, about the years spent with her husband in the apartment above the pharmacy, the reasons why she got married and those which had led to her legal separation. She and her husband, her husband and her: she spoke of nothing else. After he'd been struck down by paralysis, she explained, she'd begun to cheat on him with this or that person, because he was a sort of child, a sick child, or else a kind of old man, while she was a normal woman. The chaos of the war, with the sirens, the bombardments, every kind of fear, had certainly contributed, later, to bringing things to a head. And yet she'd always loved him, as if he were a younger brother. If she'd cheated on him, she'd done so on the quiet, taking every possible precaution. And not even that often.

It was very late when they'd mull over these conversations with Anna. Corso Roma would be so empty and silent that their voices resounded as if in a hall. Nothing else was audible, save the odd train whistle in the distance and, at every quarter hour, the chimes released into the air from the Castle clock in front.

Giorgio Bassani

There was a night, however, towards the end of August 1950, when one of these men related something new.

A little earlier, he began to tell in a low tone, he had been at Anna's house with two friends they had in common, so-and-so and such-and-such. That evening she'd been especially irritating. So much so that, at a certain point, bored that she was once again rehearsing the same old stuff, he'd interrupted her.

'A fine way to show you love your husband!' he'd cut in, laughing. 'You loved him and then went with anyone you felt like. Get away with you, you've always been big trouble!'

All hell broke loose.

'Filthy shameless cowards! Pigs!' she began yelling. 'Get the hell out of my house!'

She'd turned into a wild beast. Then the other girl, who was from Modena, she too started shouting as if she were having her throat cut. But soon enough, when apologies had been offered, both of them calmed down. And this, more or less, was what he heard soon after from Anna.

She had always loved Pino, she started saying again in her usual, tearful tone, and, in fact, for quite a few years they had come to a perfect agreement.

From the time that he could no longer walk, he spent his days in front of the dining-room window, solving one by one all the games in *Puzzles Weekly* and other magazines of that sort, for which he had a passion. He had nothing else to do – which explains why, with all those hours of practice, he'd achieved an extraordinary skill in that sort of pastime. So, sometimes, to show her how good he was, he would drag himself on his crutches to the little spiral staircase that linked to the back workroom, and from up there, leaning out over the trapdoor, he would start calling her so impatiently and insistently that she had to close the till immediately, rush upstairs and wait for him, eyes shining with pleasure, to explain how he had solved the puzzle. It was she who had to give him the long series of injections which he needed because of his illness, she who put him to bed every night before nine o'clock. What did it matter if they no longer slept together? Even before his illness he hadn't been that keen to sleep together; it made her think, actually, that he was glad to go back to sleeping alone in the little room he'd had as a boy. No, two people could sleep together all the time and not love each other at all.

However, starting from the night of 15 December 1943, everything had suddenly changed between them.

When the shooting was over she had rushed outside. Having run the length of the Giovecca, it was only at the corner of Corso Roma that she stopped for a moment to get her breath back. And while she paused under an arch of the City Theatre's portico, just there, piled up along the pavement opposite the pharmacy, she had suddenly seen the dead bodies.

She remembered every detail of the scene as if it were still before her eyes. She could see Corso Roma utterly empty under the full moon, the snow, hardened into ice, scattered like a kind of brilliant dust over everything, the air so bright and clear you could read the hour on the Castle clock – exactly twenty-one minutes past four – and finally the corpses, which from where she was looking seemed like so many bundles of rags, and yet they were human bodies, she understood that at once. Without being aware of what she was doing, she moved away from under the theatre portico, stepping out into the open towards the bodies.

It was when she was halfway there, by now in full light, and five or six metres away from the nearest heap of the dead, that the thought of Pino had crossed her mind. So she turned. And Pino was up there, motionless behind the panes of the dining-room window, a barely visible shadow that was watching her.

They remained like that, staring, for some moments, he from the dark of the room, she from the street; and her not knowing what she should do.

Finally she decided, and entered the house.

While she climbed up the spiral staircase, she tried to think what would be the best thing to tell him. It wouldn't have been too hard for her to invent some nonsense, to act in such a way that Pino believed it. He was a child, and she, in the end, was his mother.

And yet on that occasion, Pino didn't let her invent any nonsense excuse. When she came into the dining-room, he was no longer there. Instead he was in his little room, in bed, with his face turned to the wall and the covers drawn up to his ears; and to judge from the way he was breathing you would have thought him asleep. To wake him up, it's true, that would have been the right thing to do! But what if he really were asleep, and what if all she had seen from the street, just before, had been a hallucination?

In a state of doubt she had gently closed the door and had gone back to her own room, where she threw herself on the bed. She thought that in a very few hours, if not from Pino's mouth, at least from her own face, the truth would be known. And yet that wasn't to be. Not a word from him, not a look that would help her understand. Not that morning, not ever after.

Why all of this, why? If he'd been awake, why had he never admitted it? Was he afraid? But of whom precisely, of what? As far as the appearance of their relationship went, nothing had changed. Except from that time on, obsessed with his field glasses, he would pass the days surveying the pavement opposite and without ever again calling her upstairs as he once did, to show her how brilliantly he'd solved his puzzles and crosswords.

He would snigger and mutter to himself. Had he gone mad? That was a possibility, considering the disease he had. But on the other hand, how could she keep living with him without, little by little, becoming mad herself?

read more

PENGUIN MODERN CLASSICS

THE GOLD-RIMMED SPECTACLES
GIORGIO BASSANI

'A tiny unguarded moment had cost him very dear. From then on, you can imagine, he feared ridicule more than ever'

In the insular town of Ferrara, a new doctor arrives. Fadigati is hopeful and modern, and more than anything wants to fit into his new home. But his fresh, appealing appearance soon crumbles when the young man he pays to be his lover reveals the doctor's homosexuality in a public humiliation.

The second book in Bassani's *Romanzo di Ferrara* series, *The Gold-Rimmed Spectacles* is a gripping and tragic study of the terrifying historical realities that can shatter the course of individual lives.

'Elegant, elegiac . . . Jamie McKendrick's translation accurately captures Bassani's lucid, luminous style' *Guardian*

www.penguin.com

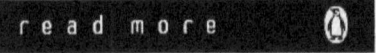

PENGUIN MODERN CLASSICS

THE GARDEN OF THE FINZI-CONTINIS
GIORGIO BASSANI

A new translation by Jamie McKendrick

'One of the great novelists of the last century' *Guardian*

Aristocratic, rich and seemingly aloof, the Finzi-Contini family fascinate the narrator of this tale, a young Jew in the Italian city of Ferrara. But it is not until he is a student in 1938, when anti-Semitic legislation is enforced on the eve of the Second World War, that he is invited into their luxurious estate.

As their gardens become a haven for persecuted Jews, the narrator becomes entwined in the lives of the family, and particularly close to Micòl, their daughter. Many years after the war has ended, he reflects on his memories of the Finzi-Continis, his experiences of love and loss and the fate of the family and community in the horrors of war.

read more

PENGUIN MODERN CLASSICS

THE SMELL OF HAY
GIORGIO BASSANI

'Down there at the very end of the corridor – at the sunlit point where its blackened walls converge – is life, vivid and throbbing as it once was'

These haunting stories set in the Jewish-Italian community of 1930s Ferrara evoke a lost world. A young man's unrequited love; a strange disappearance; a faded hotel; a lonely funfair; the smell of mown hay at the gates of the Jewish cemetery – these vivid, impressionistic snapshots build a picture of life's fragility and intensity. The last book of the *Romanzo di Ferrara* sequence, *The Smell of Hay* is told with a voice that is by turns intimate, ironic, elegiac and rueful, and features people and places from preceding novels.

This new translation by Jamie McKendrick contains two pieces, added by Bassani to his earlier collection, which have never appeared in English before.

With an introduction by Ali Smith

www.penguin.com

*Contemporary ... Provocative ... Outrageous ...
Prophetic ... Groundbreaking ... Funny ... Disturbing ...
Different ... Moving ... Revolutionary ... Inspiring ...
Subversive ... Life-changing ...*

What makes a modern classic?

At Penguin Classics our mission has always been to make the best books ever written available to everyone. And that also means constantly redefining and refreshing exactly what makes a 'classic'. That's where Modern Classics come in. Since 1961 they have been an organic, ever-growing and ever-evolving list of books from the last hundred (or so) years that we believe will continue to be read over and over again.

They could be books that have inspired political dissent, such as *Animal Farm*. Some, like *Lolita* or *A Clockwork Orange*, may have caused shock and outrage. Many have led to great films, from *In Cold Blood* to *One Flew Over the Cuckoo's Nest*. They have broken down barriers – whether social, sexual, or, in the case of *Ulysses*, the boundaries of language itself. And they might – like *Goldfinger* or *Scoop* – just be pure classic escapism. Whatever the reason, Penguin Modern Classics continue to inspire, entertain and enlighten millions of readers everywhere.

'No publisher has had more influence on reading habits than Penguin'
Independent

'Penguins provided a crash course in world literature'
Guardian

The best books ever written

PENGUIN CLASSICS

SINCE 1946

Find out more at www.penguinclassics.com